BOB DYLAN IN THE BIG APPLE

TROUBADOUR TALES OF NEW YORK

K G MILES

Published by McNidder & Grace
21 Bridge Street
Carmarthen
SA31 3JS
Wales, UK

www.mcnidderandgrace.com

Original paperback first published in 2022
© K G Miles

All rights reserved. No part of this work may be reproduced or transmitted in any form or by any means, electronic or mechanical, including photocopy, recording, or any information storage or retrieval system, without permission in writing from the publisher.

K G Miles has asserted his right to be identified as the author of this work in accordance with the Copyright, Designs and Patents Act 1988.

Every effort has been made to obtain necessary permission with reference to copyright material. The publisher apologises if, inadvertently, any sources remain unacknowledged and will be glad to make the necessary arrangements at the earliest opportunity.

A catalogue record for this work is available from the British Library.

Photographs by Gareth Davies Photography, Tenby
www.garethdaviesphotographytenby.co.uk

ISBN: 9780857162205
Ebook: 9780857162212

Designed by JS Typesetting Ltd, Porthcawl
Cover design: Tabitha Palmer
Map design: Tabitha Palmer
Cover photograph: Gareth Davies Photography, Tenby

To Jackie –

Finally 'Jokerman' is one of my favourite songs, but played by Dylan and the Plugz.

This book is the result of the 'Sweat, Blood and Muscle' of Team Big Apple –
K G Miles, Bret Johnson and Sarah Rabb.

CONTENTS

Foreword by Anne Margaret Daniel ... vii

Introduction: Sitting in South London, Dreaming of New York ... 1

Chapter 1: Bobby Before the Big Apple ... 5

Chapter 2: Cafe Wha? and Assorted Basket Houses ... 9

Chapter 3: 'If I can make it at Gerde's, I can make it anywhere' ... 19

Chapter 4: Talkin' Bob Dylan's Washington Square Park Blues ... 27

Chapter 5: The Music Inn by Dina Regine ... 37

Chapter 6: Hootenanny at Riverside Church ... 41

Chapter 7: Places to Stay, 'Crummy' and Otherwise ... 51

Chapter 8: A stay at Washington Square Hotel by Bret Johnson ... 59

Chapter 9:	Two Dylans at the White Horse Tavern	63
Chapter 10:	In 'the Office' at the Kettle of Fish	69
Chapter 11:	Horse and Kettle – Dylan's Village Bars by Bret Johnson	75
Chapter 12:	Talkin' Troubadour Tales with Terri Thal	83
Chapter 13:	Laughter and Fighting on Elizabeth Street	87
Chapter 14:	A.J. Weberman Speaks	93
Chapter 15:	New Beginning at the Bitter End and Bob at the Reservation	97
Chapter 16:	Talkin' Troubadour Tales with Scarlet Rivera	109
Chapter 17:	The Greatest Band You Never Saw	117
Chapter 18:	Bob at the Beacon	129
Afterword by Maureen Van Zandt		133
Final Word		137
List of photographs and map		139
Locations list		141
Bibliography		155
Acknowledgements		161
Author biography		163

FOREWORD
by Anne Margaret Daniel

'Nobody needs to ask me how I feel about this city.'
Bob Dylan, onstage at the Beacon Theatre

He arrived in New York City at the age of nineteen, either in December of 1960 or January 1961. He didn't linger on the Upper West Side, where he claimed he got out of the car right away and caught a subway train, nor in Times Square. Bob Dylan went straight to Greenwich Village. The home of artists, writers, actors, eccentrics, and progressives since the late 1800s, the Village was by 1960 the beating heart of the folk music scene. Long a home for jazz and cabarets, the Village was the logical place for young people singing old songs to gather, to share the music they had learned from John and Alan Lomax's recordings, from The Weavers, from Folkways albums. Perhaps not his first night ever in town, but soon after, Dylan played an open mic night at the Cafe Wha? – and then Gerde's Folk City – the Village Gate – the Bitter End – the

Fat Black Pussycat – the Gaslight – and, thanks to Izzy Young of the Folklore Center on MacDougal Street, the Carnegie Chapter Hall.

While he lived in the Village on the couches of kindred spirits and indulgent, admiring couples with no kids of their own, and then in his first place, a little room of one's own with 17-year-old Suze Rotolo, Dylan was a hungry, eager student. Liam Clancy, who he listened to raptly at the White Horse and who became a good friend, described him, in a good way, as 'a sponge.' Along with the stages in basements and back rooms and bars, the Folklore Center, Dave Van Ronk's and Paul Clayton's libraries, and the reading room at the New York Public Library on 5th Avenue at 42nd Street were where he was educated. He learned about art and film and politics in the Village, too, thanks largely to Rotolo. And it was on stage at Gerde's that he was noticed by *New York Times* columnist Robert Shelton, who called him 'a bright new face in folk music.... a cross between a choir boy and a beatnik,' who 'composes new songs faster than he can remember them[.]' Shelton's note was in the *Times* on 29 September, 1961. Just days later, John Hammond, Sr. signed Dylan, not yet 21, to Columbia Records. He was still a minor for purposes of signing a contract, but, Hammond later told Shelton, Dylan 'said he didn't have a manager or parents.'

Dylan began recording his albums at Columbia Studio A on 7th Avenue. *Bob Dylan* (1962) shows the shape of New York throughout: a collection of covers of the folk songs he was singing in the Village every night; one original song by the young singer-songwriter himself on each side; and a cover portrait by Michael Ochs, brother of Dylan's contemporary Phil. His next album, *The Freewheelin' Bob Dylan*, flipped the ratio of original songs to covers: eleven of the first, and among them some of his best-known compositions still, and two of the latter. He drew on the musical wealth of New York City to supplement his own traditional, solo, guitar-and-harmonica playing; his backing band in the studio were mostly jazz musicians. Don Hunstein photographed Bob and Suze together for this album's cover, around the corner from their West 4th Street apartment on a snowy Jones Street. Suze walked out of Bob's life soon after, but decades later, as Dylan performed 'Simple Twist of Fate' at the Beacon Theatre on Broadway, he sang lyrics about walking along city blocks, and wishing that the couple in the song had met in 1958 – a reminder that the song once bore the title 'Snowbound' and then '4th Street Affair.'

As his career skyrocketed, Dylan lived and stayed in the city. His new manager Albert Grossman had a home on Gramercy Park that Dylan regularly used as a crash pad and setting for photo shoots; he rented homes in midtown, in Harlem, in SoHo, and bought 92-94 MacDougal Street in a Village homecoming after years of being based up the Hudson River in Woodstock. He maintained an apartment at the Chelsea Hotel, #225, in the late 60's and early 70's. He and his wife Sara raised their children in the city at first, before moving to Malibu, California in 1973 – a move that Dylan didn't quite complete at the time, returning to New York for long stretches of time to take art classes, to record, and to organize and run the Rolling Thunder Revue. Since 1988, he has made New York and a variety of venues a regular stop on his annual tours. He still has corporate offices, and perhaps residences, in town.

Even when Dylan isn't in the city, the city is in him. Talkin' New York, carrying *The New York Times*, hard times in the city livin' down in New York town, the streets of Little Italy, down to the Bowery slums, I drove down 42nd Street in my Cadillac, escapades out on the D train, staying up for days in the Chelsea Hotel – and that heart cry of I'm goin' back to New York City / I do believe I've had enough. K G Miles, Bret Johnson, and Dina Regine have followed Dylan from young Village troubadour to Broadway Bob, in residence with his band at the Beacon Theatre most recently in December 2019 – East Side, West Side, all around the town, leaving no cobblestone unturned. Dylan's inspirations, and traces, are everywhere in New York City. Read, and see.

Anne Margaret Daniel
Woodstock, NY, August 2021

Bob Dylan in the Big Apple

'Dylan in New York. New York in Dylan. Always look up when you walk around Greenwich Village.'
Photo by Anne Margaret Daniel

INTRODUCTION

Sitting in South London, Dreaming of New York...

From the Bowery to the Bronx, from the East Village to Harlem, from Hudson Heights to Lennox Hill, and from Korea Town to Little Italy, from Hell's Kitchen to Greenwich Village, from Manhattan Valley, from Midtown South to Midtown itself... That's right we're talking about the greatest piece of real estate on the planet, the little island known as Manhattan, so settle in and join us...

Bob Dylan, Theme Time Radio, 4 April 2007

I was too young to enjoy the 1960s until the 1970s.

Like many English music fans, including a young Mark Feld who changed his surname to Bolan in homage, my introduction to Bob Dylan came with the exceedingly uncool medium of a Greatest Hits album.

Except the 1971 release *More Bob Dylan Greatest Hits*, as the double album is known in England, is far from a conventional round-up of the tried and the tested and the commercially popular. This album contained both new tracks and re-recorded tracks and the cover picture suggested it was a live album (it wasn't).

One track, however, is live and it appears suddenly, almost mystically, smack bang in the middle of Side Four. It's the previously unheard 'Tomorrow Is A Long Time', a haunting performance from a young Bob Dylan at the Carnegie Hall, which had been lying in a mythical drawer for eight years. Not only did this sound transform me from a South London bedroom to the New York of April 1963, it also sparked my journey on a Dylanista path – from which I've never strayed.

I am not a scholar. I am a fan. This book, both history and guide, provides an opportunity for me to conjure up that unique Bob Dylan and New York vibe. New York and Bob Dylan are inextricably linked. New York, and in particular Greenwich Village in the early 1960s, was a creative melting pot. Very much the right place and the right time for a young Robert Zimmerman to be reborn and to blossom as Bob Dylan.

By following in Bob's footsteps, the music tourist can use this guide to watch performances in Washington Square Park, drink at the Kettle of Fish before finally laying a weary head at the renamed and refurbished Hotel Earle. No heating pipes will 'cough'.

We will stop at extraordinary places and meet some remarkable characters who helped to form the Dylan story:

George Margolin, the maverick printer, whose single, extraordinary act paved the way for all New York folksingers. A man so hitherto forgotten to history that not only does his pioneering have no statue or a plaque in commemoration, but there isn't even a grainy, iconic photograph to pass down.

Ramblin' Jack Elliott, the folksinger and Dylan mentor over decades, whose Woody Guthrie style was the real template for the young Bobby.

Karen Dalton, the singer Dylan described as his favourite. A singer who shared a stage with Dylan in his very early days at the Cafe Wha? but whose career went in completely the opposite direction to Bob.

Throughout the decades New York has been a constant stage for Dylan. From the Cafe Wha? to the Beacon Theatre, we will pause just briefly along the way to introduce you to the Greatest Band You Never Saw.

Bob Dylan in the Big Apple is, as Dylan sang in 'Hard Times In New York Town', 'just a little glimpse of a story I'll tell'. To provide a fully comprehensive look at Bob Dylan in New York would require a book so voluminous that the music tourist would require an accompanying wheelbarrow. So leave your wheelbarrow in the shed and join me as we take in the sound of *Desire*, get a first-hand account of fighting in the street, meet Avril the Dancer and encounter a fellow named Dolores.

Chapter 1
BOBBY BEFORE THE BIG APPLE

I grew up as a young music fan knowing only two unassailable facts. That Bob Dylan was born in Duluth, Minnesota and that Video Killed the Radio Star. Ironically it was Bob who cast doubt upon both.

'I was born in Duluth, Minnesota or maybe it was Superior, Wisconsin.'

The history of the young Robert Allen Zimmerman, before he headed to New York where Bob Dylan was officially 'born', was shrouded for a long time in a fog of his own making.

Even the official program for his Carnegie Chapter Hall concert in 1961 continued to spin the young folksinger's yarns: 'Bob Dylan was born in Duluth, Minnesota in 1941. He was raised in Gallup, New Mexico and before he came to New York earlier this year, he lived in Iowa, South Dakota, North Dakota and Kansas. He started playing carnivals at the age of fourteen on guitar and piano.'

Only the date and the place of his birth were correct … oh, and he was a pretty mean guitar and piano player at a young age.

We have a reasonably good idea that Bob Dylan hitched a ride to New York City on Tuesday, 24 January 1961. Reinvention had been a part of the Greenwich Village life long before Dylan arrived. Suze Rotolo, who was to become his mentor, his muse and his partner throughout much of his early career in New York, said in her memoir that 'everyone had come to the Village to find or lose themselves.'

Dave Van Ronk, a folksinger already in the Village when young Bobby arrived and a huge support to him throughout the years, said it was perfectly acceptable to fabricate a previous life once you hit Greenwich Village. 'Nobody held it against him. Reinventing yourself has always been part of show business. But he sort of got backed into a corner with his own story. I remember he solemnly gave us a demonstration of Indian sign language which he was obviously making up as he went along.'

Dylan told friends in the Village that he used to play for the rock 'n' roll star Bobby Vee, occasionally extending this to getting friends to point him out to strangers as the actual Bobby Vee!

In 1966 he told biographer Robert Shelton, who took most of the stories with a shaker of salt, that he spent the first two months in New York hustling as a male prostitute: 'we hustled for two months, sometimes we would make $150 or $250 a night between us and hang around in cars, cats would pick us up and chicks would pick us up. We would do anything they wanted … I almost got killed.'

Bob was keen to spin a fanciful yarn about his history. Here's what he told *Playboy* magazine in 1966:

> *I lost my one true love. I started drinking … I woke up in a pool hall. Then this big Mexican lady drags me off the table, takes me to Philadelphia, she leaves me alone in her house, and it burns down, I wind up in Phoenix … I got a job as a 'before' in a Charles Atlas 'Before and After' ad … Next thing I know I'm in Omaha … I move in with a high school teacher who also does a little plumbing on the side, who has a special kind of refrigerator that can turn newspaper into lettuce. Everything's going fine until that delivery boy shows up … he burned the house down and I hit the road. The first guy that picked me up asked if I wanted to be a star. What could I say?'*
>
> *Playboy: And that's how you became a rock 'n' roll singer?'*
>
> *No, that's how I got tuberculosis.*

Thankfully over the years, the fog of mystery has been carefully lifted by the wonderful Dylan books covering his early years, by the writers Anthony Scaduto, Robert Shelton and Toby Thompson. We have comprehensive accounts of a very ordinary, comfortable upbringing in a lovely Jewish family in Minnesota – no tuberculosis, no carnivals.

Young Robert Zimmerman was heading to New York to visit his dying musical hero, Woody Guthrie, in the hospital. 'I'm going to New York,' he told his friends. 'I am going to see Woody and I'm going to make it big.'

In his autobiography, *Chronicles*, Dylan describes arriving in New York and taking 'a rockin', a reelin', a rollin', ride on the subway.' It is likely he actually walked.

Chapter 2
CAFE WHA? AND ASSORTED BASKET HOUSES

For any young music fan growing up in the '60s and '70s, there are a small number of venues whose very name convey a magical place. New York's Madison Square Garden, LA's Troubadour … and in Croydon, South London, The Greyhound.

'A four door Pontiac is just leaving the Hudson Tunnel. It has carried five people from Madison, Wisconsin to New York City. It's late afternoon on Tuesday 24 January, 1961 and the snow is driving across the highway. The windscreen wipers are flipping and flapping too slowly to properly clear the snowflakes. The car is warm, and New York is cold.' Thus, the scene is set by John Bauldie, the English Dylan expert. Bauldie tells us that one of the passengers in the car is a young Bob Dylan. Dylan, whether he took the rockin' and reelin' subway or he walked, knew exactly where he was headed. To the Cafe Wha?

As Dylan outlines in his beautifully written but somewhat fanciful autobiography, 'the place was a subterranean cavern, liquorless, ill lit, low ceiling, like a wide dining hall with chairs and tables – open at noon, closed at four in the morning. Somebody had told me to go there and ask for a singer named Freddy Neil who ran the daytime show at the Wha?'

It was certainly the right place for Dylan to be. Robert Shelton, the writer who was soon to be reviewing Dylan at these venues, commented that 'for a time, the hottest scene was in a basement boite called the Cafe Wha? The manager, Manny Roth, was always offering jobs to young musicians who drifted in.'

Manny Roth always had a good eye for a good thing. In 1959 someone had told Manny Roth about a garage that used to be an old horse stable on MacDougal Street between Bleecker and West 3rd Street. It was down deep stairs and, according to the Cafe Wha? website, was a 'dark, dank basement which was bisected by a trough once used as a gutter for horse dung.' The visionary Manny Roth 'immediately recognized it as an excellent site for a coffee house – that legendary genre of cafe where, at least in the haziness of memory, hipsters smoked, sipped espresso and discussed Sartre.'

> Dylan, whether he took the rockin' and reelin' subway or walked, knew exactly where he was headed – to the Cafe Wha?
>
> **Map ref. 7**

By the time Dylan arrived, that vision was somewhat tempered. It was a 'basket house' folk venue. At a packed-out session, it could hold 325 and the performer could survive by passing around a cap, thus an early and vital prop for Dylan: 'you passed the basket … that's why I started wearing hats.' On Tuesday, 24 January, 1961, when Dylan arrived at Cafe Wha?, he immediately struck lucky. It was Hootenanny night – an open mic session when pretty much anyone could get up and perform.

Maddy Bloom, a waitress at the time, recalled the arrival of the young Dylan. He told her he was 'Followin' in Woody Guthrie's footsteps. Going to the places he went to. "All I got is my guitar and that little knapsack. That's all I need." I remember thinking he was very raw, that he had no professional polish, but that he had a quality of such innocence, in a way, that you just had to listen to him and watch him.' Looking back in 1984, Dylan said of the experience, 'if they didn't like you back then, you couldn't play! If they liked you, you played more. And if they didn't like you, you didn't play at all. You played one or two songs and people would just boo or hiss or something.'

Dylan settled well on the New York stage. He had a charm and a humour that quickly endeared him to audiences. As Dylan recalled, 'it was a nonstop flow of people. Usually, they were tourists who were looking for beatniks in the Village.' He really took to the place even though he tells us in *Chronicles* that the 'acts were disjointed, awkward … the audience was mostly collegiate types, suburbanites, lunch-hour secretaries, sailors and tourists.' The daytime show was 'an extravaganza patchwork … a comedian, a ventriloquist, a steel drum group, a poet, a female impersonator, a duo who sang Broadway, a rabbit-in-the-hat magician, a guy wearing a turban who hypnotized people in the audience, somebody who's entire act was facial acrobatics.'

The Cafe Wha? was an entertainment education for Dylan. However, on 24 January 1961, there were three more pressing reasons for venturing to the venue and to settle in. Firstly, it was out of the biting cold of a New York winter. Secondly, it was a venue that fed the performers. Dylan described the food as 'actually the best thing about the place' and soon became very dependent on 'all the French fries and hamburgers I could eat' provided by Norbert the cook. A starving Tiny Tim would often join Dylan in the food queue. The other important element that the Cafe Wha? gave Dylan, then sofa surfing, was a place to stay. He told Manny Roth that he 'just got here from the west. Name's Bob Dylan. I'd like to do a few songs. Can I?' Manny Roth introduced him as a such from the stage – and in the traditional folk scene fashion, he also asked if there was anywhere for the young singer to stay. In a 1961 interview for Columbia Records, Dylan says that there were a few offers. With a friend, probably Mark Spoelstra who had travelled with him to New York, they picked a fellow out of the audience. 'He looks okay – and anyway he was with a girl, and so we went up to him. And the girl got off at

34th Street, and we got off at 42nd Street! Well, we went to a bar before we went to find this place to stay. And we met his gentleman friend, Dolores. Dolores was a friend who stayed with him. And both of us looked and ran out of the bar!' The boys from Minnesota weren't quite ready for New York's rich tapestry.

Where Dylan actually stayed that first night is, like so much of his early time in New York, shrouded in mystery. There have been suggestions that he spent some time sleeping in the subway, but that is unlikely. Even at this early stage, Dylan was a very accomplished 'schnorrer', a Yiddish term for somebody who mooches for a living. He was soon established as the harmonica accompaniment to Fred Neil, described by Dylan as the 'Emperor of the place, even had his own harem, his devotees.' As Dylan recalled in 1984, 'I used to play with a guy called Fred Neil, who wrote the song "Everybody's Talkin'" that was in the film *Midnight Cowboy*.' (Chosen, ironically, because the first choice, a song called 'Lay, Lady Lay' by a certain Bob Dylan, was recorded too late.) 'I would play harmonica for him, and then, once in a while, get to sing a song, you know when he was taking a break or something. It was his show, he would be on for about half an hour, then a conga group would get on, called Los Congueros, with twenty conga drummers and bongos and steel drums.'

There is a beautiful photograph taken at the Cafe Wha? in those early days featuring Dylan, in waistcoat and trademark folksinger cap, playing harmonica for

Fred Neil. The third person joining them on stage, in what looks like a joyous jam session, is one of the first singers Dylan played with in New York. A folk singer described by Dylan in *Chronicles* as his favorite singer at that time in New York. A singer who 'had a voice like Billie Holiday's and played the guitar like Jimmy Reed.' That singer was Karen Dalton.

Often pictured with Dylan and the small group of friends he quickly found in New York, Karen Dalton had a remarkable voice and was an extraordinary talent. Her fellow performer on that Cafe Wha? stage, Fred Neil said of Karen Dalton in his liner notes for her 1971 album *In My Own Time* that 'Karen was like a letter from home. Her voice is so unique, to describe it would take a poem. All I can say is she sure can sing the shit out of the blues.' Poetic indeed.

A Cherokee who, like so many, drifted into New York, Karen was one of those artists in Greenwich Village blessed with a raw passion and talent … And who like so many burned brightly, then slowly dimmed.

Part of Karen Dalton's unique voice, described once as the sound of grain and sand, was due to the loss, before she arrived on the New York folk scene, of her two bottom teeth. Her daughter, Abralyn Baird, recalled in 2008 that 'the man she was living with at the time, he came home and found her in bed with my soon-to-be stepfather, and yeah, a fight ensued. She got punched in the face. She always said when she got that big recording contract and became famous, she was gonna have teeth put in.'

A recording contract came – but success didn't. While Dylan was making his way to the top, Karen, like so many in the Greenwich Village folk scene, was gradually sliding to the bottom. She died in a trailer in Hurley outside Woodstock in 1993. By then, she had lived with AIDS for ten years. Her close friend Peter Walker and her son Jonny Lee looked after her towards the end. Thankfully, her talent was not forgotten, certainly not by Dylan. It is said that the song 'Katie's Been Gone', by Dylan and The Band and featured on *The Basement Tapes*, was about her. Other singers, such as Nick Drake, have sited her as an influence. In recent years, Charlotta Hayes, whose documentary is due out in 2023, has kept the legacy of Karen Dalton from completely disappearing from view. Karen left few songs and so little video. Then one day in 2004 a performance from a festival in Europe suddenly appeared online. As the Calle Si Blogspot of 2021 excitedly reported, '… a few days ago one of the few videos in which Karen Dalton can be seen playing live came to light. Recorded at the Golden Rose Pop Festival in the year 1971, it shows the Texan artist in one of those extraordinary moments in which she received well deserved applause of the public. It also shows why she never burst out of the limited, limiting cult status. During the brief performance she barely looks away from the stage … and then she leaves the stage with no ceremony.'

This video of Karen Dalton appeared as if by magic one day on YouTube … then – and, sadly, fittingly – it was gone. (As this book goes to press the documentary, *Karen Dalton: In My Own Time* by Richard Peete and Robert Yapkowitz has been released in the US and worldwide to follow. This documentary shows Karen as a complex and extraordinary artist.)

Bob Dylan had no such difficulty in shining on stage. From the Cafe Wha?, he began to circulate throughout the lively Greenwich Village folk circuit.

There were many basket houses, coffee houses, folk clubs and assorted venues that Dylan frequented in those early years. One of these was the Gaslight Cafe where a fellow Greenwich Village Troubadour, John Winn recalls: 'I sat in a booth one day in '61 and listened to Bobby Dylan spin his imaginary stories of life on the road as an orphan which all of us had to take with a shaker full of salt.' Dylan was established quickly on the folk scene and the Gaslight Cafe was next on the ambitious youngster's target list. As he recalls in *Chronicles*, 'I kept my eye on the Gaslight, how could I not?'

It is said that the 20-year-old Dylan approached Hugh Romney (known later and known widely as Wavy Gravy) who hosted their hootenanny nights to ask whether he could perform. Romney wasted no time, going to the mic and saying, 'there he is, a legend in his own lifetime … uh … what's your name, kid?' One of the main differences between the Gaslight and the other basket houses was that the performers didn't have to pass their own hat or basket around. At the Gaslight, this task was undertaken by Malcolm the Witch, a green-haired lady with a python in a bag. Perhaps a little extra incentive to pay up and maybe a large part of the reason that at one point Dylan was being paid $75 a week.

The Gaslight has apartments above with air shafts down to the club so that at one point the police stopped the nuisance of the sound of applause filtering up. Performers who did well were greeted with approving click of the fingers. Artists would play poker upstairs and there were speakers so that when it was their turn, they could grab their guitar and run downstairs. The Gaslight would not only be an impor-

> The Gaslight would not only be an important venue for Dylan to hone his stage craft; in 1963 it was where he met Johnny Cash.
>
> **Map ref. 6**

tant venue for Dylan to hone his stage craft; in 1963 it was where he met Johnny Cash. On 6 September, 1961 it was where Dylan premiered two of his most famous songs. One of them was 'Masters of War.' The other began life in the rooms above the Gaslight as the folksinger Tom Paxton recalled in 2000: 'there was a hideout room above the Gaslight where we could hang out. Once, Dylan was out banging this poem on Wavy

Gravy's typewriter. He showed me the poem and I asked, "Is this a song?" He said, "No, it's a poem." I said, "All this work and you're not going to add a melody?" He did. It was "A Hard Rain's a-Gonna Fall".'

Chapter 3
'IF I CAN MAKE IT AT GERDE'S, I CAN MAKE IT ANYWHERE'

It is only human nature to seek out the bright lights, to seek a stage on which to shine. In the distance for a young Bob Dylan was the spotlight on the stage at one of the most important of all of the folk music venues in Greenwich Village, Gerde's Folk City. Dylan said if he could make it at Gerde's, he could 'make it anywhere'. Howard Sounes, Dylan biographer, describes this important venue thus: 'by day the club was a traditional Italian restaurant with floral wallpaper and a jukebox loaded with Frank Sinatra records. At night Mike Porco, who spoke English like Groucho Marx, presides over what became known as the best folk club in New York.' Mike Porco's grandson Bob describes him with a classic New York phrase: 'he was the straw that stirred the drink'.

The club began life just as much of the 1960s Greenwich Village folk scene did, with the tour de force that was Izzy Young. He began a folk night called the Fifth Peg. Club owner Mike Porco soon saw a pretty decent buck to be made and quickly cut poor Izzy out of the equation by enticing a young entrepreneur, Charles Rothschild, a regular at the White Horse Tavern. So only two months after the launch of the Fifth Peg, it was relaunched on 30 May 1960, with the folksinger Carolyn Hester.

Dylan knew Gerde's was the place he needed to play, and it was to become a venue that accelerated his career.

Liam Clancy was urging Mike Porco to book the young Dylan, but as often happened in those early days, it was one of the mother hens who came to Dylan's aid. Dylan could, most Sundays, be found in the company of Woody Guthrie and others. Barbara Shutner was there with her husband, Logan English. As Barbara said in 1961, 'In came this funny looking kid one night, dressed as if he had just spent a year riding freight trains and playing songs in a style that you could tap your feet to.' Logan English was impressed by the scruffy youngster providing Sunday entertainment to Woody Guthrie. 'I'm working at Gerde's. I'm the MC. We'll get

> Dylan knew Gerde's was the place he needed to play, and it was to become a venue that accelerated his career.
> **Map ref. 12**

you to play there.' Logan put in a good word for Dylan but it was the perseverance of Terri Thal that secured the historic booking. As Terri recalls 'Mike and I met a few times to discuss whether Bob was ready to perform there; at our second meeting he agreed to bring Bob in.' Dylan played his first major gig there, opening for John Lee Hooker on 13 February 1961. According to *New York* magazine, he played 'House of the Rising Sun', 'Song to Woody', 'Talkin' Hava Negeilah Blues', 'Black Blues' and a Woody Guthrie song that no one can recall with certainty. Dylan took very naturally to the bigger stage. As Barbara Shutner recalled, 'Dylan's style was a combination of blues, rock and country which caught on the minute that he stepped on the stage at Gerde's.' It was a combination that would continue to entrance audiences for the next fifty years and beyond.

However, the inexorable rise of Bob Dylan was almost derailed only two months into his Gerde's residence. To keep playing, Dylan needed to apply for a Union card. Mike Porco took him to the union office on 3 April 1961: 'The man gave Bob the Union card, Dylan couldn't complete the form…' He was only 19. 'And as the Union man said, "I can't OK this because you're under 21. Come in tomorrow with your father." "I ain't got no father," said Dylan. "Well, come in with your mother." "I ain't got no mother." The Union man leans back behind Dylan and forms the words with his mouth "Is he a bastard?" And I said, "I don't know." Then he suggested I sign it as a guardian. And I did. Bob got his Union book.'

At this point Mike Porco gave him some of his kid's clothes and got Bob a haircut.

Looking back in 1965 in 'The Charisma Kid,' Robert Shelton, who is to play a further very important role in the career of Dylan, and indeed this chapter, gave a wonderfully florid account of Dylan at that time:

> *He was only 19 then, looking, with his thin pale face, as if parts of a choirboy and parts of a beatnik had gone astray in one of the tunnels from Jersey and hastily reassembled before the Manhattan exit. In the Village clubs, Dylan touched his audience occasionally with his bluesy songs and his emerging poetic statements, but mostly he made them laugh. He had a curious set of Charlie Chaplin Tramp mannerisms that were irresistible. His shamble would send him way past the target of the microphone and there was a lot of stage business with his hat, his hair, his harmonica.*

Gerde's was the venue where Dylan met many people who were important to him or became important to his career. One who was very much both of those was Joan Baez. Speaking in 1995 she recalled: 'I was at Gerde's maybe three or four times. I never did a gig there officially. I sang with Bob a couple of times impromptu. And that's also where I met him and saw him for the first time.' Baez was smart enough to see through the image to the talent within. 'As I remember him, it seems that he was about five feet, he seemed tiny, just tiny with that goofy little hat on ... And he was just astounding. I'm really hooked on geniuses and at any time it happens along, I really get excited.'

There were also two performers at Gerde's who meant a great deal to Dylan the folk troubadour, Dylan the artist continuing the great American folk tradition. Both had an important connection to Woody Guthrie. Dylan would meet one briefly, while the other would be an occasional companion to Dylan for many years. Cisco Houston had met Woody Guthrie in California in 1939. Cisco recalled, 'We travelled up and down California together in the fruit pickers camps and saloons.' Just as Dylan was primarily in New York to meet his hero Woody Guthrie, so too was Woody impressed when he first met Cisco. In his 1943 autobiography *Bound for Glory*, he explained: 'I ran into a guitar playing partner standing on a bad corner, and he called hisself The Cisco Kid. He was a long-legged guy that walked like he was on a rowing ship, a good singer and a yodeler, and he had sailed the seas a lot of times. Busted labels in a lot of ports and had really been around in his twenty-six years.' Woody joined Cisco in sailing the seas in the Merchant Navy.

When Dylan arrived in New York, Cisco was already dying of cancer but, unlike the terminally sick Woody Guthrie, had a matter of only a very few months left. Clearly it was a real honour for Dylan to meet Cisco. Looking back in 1984, Dylan recalls 'one of the biggest thrills I actually had was when I reached New York ... and I got to play with Cisco Houston. I think

I got to play with him at a party someplace. But I used to watch him, he used to play at Folk City. He was an amazing looking guy. He looked like Clark Gable, like a movie star.' As with many of the Greenwich Village talents, Dylan bemoans Cisco's lack of recognition. 'He was one of the unsung heroes, one of the great American figures of all time, but yet you can ask people about him and nobody knows anything about him.' Cisco died on 29 April 1961, but only after one last performance at Gerde's. As described in '*Hoot!: A Twenty-Five Year History of the Greenwich Folk Scene*' by Robbie Woliver, 'one dramatic night at Folk City was the last performance of Cisco Houston. He could literally hardly stand on his feet, but he wanted to go on with his engagement. A whole bunch of us came down for that show – the Weavers, the Tarriers, Pete Seeger, Arlo (Guthrie) and Bobby Dylan was there.' Cisco was said, in *Sing Out!* magazine in 1961, to have 'walked with grace through an imperfect world.'

The other Woody Guthrie compadre that Dylan met at the time and who became a long-time companion was Ramblin' Jack Elliot. Ramblin' Jack had spent the mid-1950s busking around Europe with Derroll Adams. They were the first to bring American folk music to those streets. This so inspired one young somebody, he went out the next day to buy a guitar. That somebody was Mick Jagger. One of the first people Ramblin' Jack encountered on returning from Europe was Bob Dylan. As Ramblin' Jack recalled in 1998, 'I met him while we were visiting Woody in the hospital. This was in 1961.' Dylan was in New York 'mostly still doing a lot of traditional songs, great old Jimmie Rodgers' songs, railroad blues, most everybody couldn't stand his voice because it was out of control, and he was gone through puberty. Couldn't even grow a beard. He was a cute kid, though. He looked like a poet.'

Both Bob and Ramblin' Jack had a devotion to Woody Guthrie. So much so, that Ramblin' Jack once said, 'my wives always mentioned Woody Guthrie in the papers as a reason why they would divorce me.' However, there was something else that Ramblin' Jack and Bob Dylan had in common – as Dave Van Ronk recalled, 'as far as Bobby knew, Jack Elliott was absolutely gold coin goyisha cowboy … it came out somehow that he was Elliott Adnopoz, a Jewish cat from Ocean Parkway and Bobby fell off his chair. He rolled under the table laughing like a madman … we had suspected Bobby was Jewish, and that proved it.'

Dylan, who was sometimes referred to as 'the son of Jack Elliot', remained a close friend. He even appeared on the 'Rollin' Thunder Revue' and sang in Dylan's film *Renaldo and Clara*. Both continued to sing.

The Rolling Thunder Revue was given an impromptu launch on the night of Mike Porco's 61st birthday, just before the circus rolled out of town. Allen Ginsberg later commented that 'the folk era had died' then – adding, with the twinkle that was so often in his eye, 'or had it?'

The original Gerde's moved to 3rd Street in the 1970s and closed in the late 1980s. On the site now, there stands – fittingly for Elliot Adnopoz and Robert Zimmerman – the Hebrew Union College, the Jewish Institute of Religion.

All of the above would be enough for Gerde's Folk City to hold a special place in Dylan history. However, it is one moment on 29 September 1961, reviewed by Robert Shelton review for the *New York Times*, that gets Gerde's a place in musical folklore. Shelton said very little about the main act, the Greenbriar Boys, instead focusing on a 'bright new face in folk music who was appearing at Gerde's Folk City'. Shelton said that Dylan resembled a 'cross between a choirboy and a beatnik' and that a 'searing intensity pervades his songs'. He concludes that 'his music making has the mark of originality and inspiration, all the more noteworthy for his youth. Mr. Dylan is vague about his antecedents and birthplace, but it matters less where he has been that where he is going.'

After this review, Mr. Dylan was going only one way.

Chapter 4
TALKIN' BOB DYLAN'S WASHINGTON SQUARE PARK BLUES

In 1969, rather than walk down the road to the festival in his own backyard at Woodstock, Dylan headed to a festival on an island off the coast of England, the Isle of Wight. As a small child accompanied by my maverick auntie, I joined him on the island. I was too young to enjoy the music or appreciate the immensity of the event. My only abiding memory is of the strange, multicoloured, overly fantastical, 'hippy' creatures who surrounded me. Where did they come from? From which exotic and hedonistic planet had they descended on to this island? Only many years later did I find out that the centre of their beautiful planet was called Greenwich Village.

Way back in 1943, Allen Ginsberg wrote to his brother Eugene saying, 'Saturday I plan to go down to Greenwich Village with a friend of mine who claims to be an "intellectual" and knows queer and interesting people there. I plan to get drunk Saturday evening if I can.'

In the middle of Greenwich Village sits Washington Square Park, a location with a haunting history from rather worse times. Just east of today's fountain were the gallows while the potter's field was originally the burial place of yellow fever victims, prostitutes, criminals, the unnamed, the indigent – and many, many African Americans (who also had a village on the site under the Dutch called Little Africa, when this part of the Village still lay far north of city limits). The field then became a drill field and parade ground for the 7th Regiment. Throughout the last two centuries, coffins and bones have found their way to the surface too – around 20,000 bodies are said to lie below the winding paths and playgrounds.

The counterculture roots were firmly planted in the 1900s, when avant-garde ideas in literature, art, sexual experimentation, freedom and politics blossomed. Here was an American Bohemia where all of these elements flourished – apart from music. Not, at least, until George Margolin arrived. George changed everything.

People's Songs was a group formed on 31 December 1945. Pete Seeger was installed as Chairman with the rallying cry, 'The people are on the march and must have songs to sing, now in 1946 the truth must reassert itself in many singing voices.'

The group took offices on 130 West 42nd Street. They set up to run a booking agency, and its newsletter outlined that its 'first job was to write verses for a song voicing the feelings of soldiers overseas' and copies were sent to protesting GIs in Manila. Newsletters were printed, songs were written, and committees were formed. At the first meeting, the 41 members were divided into a temporary organising committee and advisory committee. What the People's Songs weren't doing, however, was singing to the people. Washington Square Park is described in Dan Drasin's short film documentary *Sunday* (2013), now part of the permanent film collection at New York's Museum of Modern Art, as '8 acres of everybody's front porch. In the old days, they used to gather around to watch hangings.' After the Second World War, the hangings had long stopped but nothing terribly exciting happened … until along came George Margolin.

George Margolin was a commercial printer by trade. In the spring of 1946 (although some say 1945 and some even say 1947), George took it entirely upon himself to sing in the park one Sunday. According to Ramblin' Jack Elliott George 'simply ambled around the park and sang a capella' in a solo show of 'tuneful eccentricity'. Soon George began taking his guitar on a Sunday.

As described by the Newton Community website, 'one summer afternoon in 1945, a young guitar player named George Margolin wandered through Washington Square. Someone requested a song and he obliged; soon a small crowd gathered around him … Participants enjoyed the experience so much that they agreed to meet again the following Sunday. They continued each week…'

Neil Rosenberg, in *Bluegrass: A History*, tells us that among George's first set lists were the folk songs 'Brown Eyes', 'Midnight Special', 'Cindy', and the mystically titled, 'I Ride an Old Paint.'

If the timing of George's revolutionary amble is shrouded in mystery, so is his background and his fate.

According to many sources, including Ramblin' Jack Elliott, this 'commercial printer became a member of People's Songs, a loose knit collection of politically left-tilting singers and songwriters in a Greenwich Village basement.' However, although the 41 members listed in the first People's Songs minutes include not just Pete Seeger but such folk luminaries such as Woody Guthrie and Burl Ives, there is no sign of George Margolin. George had simply taken it upon himself to take folk music to the people, his lone act sparking folksinging in Greenwich Village.

The success of George's Sunday folksinging in the park soon filtered down to the People's Songs' basement office. Pete Seeger and his fellow 'left-tilting' songwriters soon realised that the maverick troubadour George was really onto something with his Sunday in the park singalongs. Pete Seeger applied for the appropriate licence to perform in the park and the rest is, as they may have said, singing social history.

By 1947 the rogue George was featured in the *People's Songs Vol. 2* as the originator of the 'Sidewalk Hootenanny'. George has made it on to the same pages as Woody and Pete. After kickstarting this folk music tradition … we never hear from George again.

Very quickly, as writer Sean Wilentz noted, 'flocks of folk instrumentalists and singers of every variety crowded the dry fountain at the center of the square.' One of the troubadour contemporaries of Dylan and, like Bob, still composing and performing is the formidable John Winn. He describes the scene on a Sunday in the park thus: 'fiddles, assorted wind instruments, drums of many varieties, mandolins, kazoos, exotic like nose flutes, jaw harps, pigeons cooing, harmonicas, autoharps, balalaikas – a cacophony of sound that would coalesce in groups.' In John Winn's time, this Sunday throng was often joined by the 'tall apparition' of a character called Moondog. 'His lanky frame was wrapped in flowing robes with a horned Viking helmet topping off his imperial costume. When he majestically made his way through the park, people stepped aside as if he was Moses parting the waters.' There is no statue to the pioneering George Margolin. As folksinging in Greenwich Village grew rapidly, the singing printer drifted into almost complete historical oblivion.

By the time Dylan arrived in Greenwich Village, the folk scene was so lively, it was starting to come to the attention of the very conservative American mainstream, and they didn't like what they saw. In 1961, the columnist Walter Winchell told the following apocryphal and humourous story: 'A policeman accosted a suspicious looking stroller in the square and demanded to know what he was doing there. "I'm looking for someone to mug," the suspect confessed. "Sorry," the officer apologized, "I thought you were a folk singer."'

Dan Drasin's short film *Sunday*, is a record of the moment the blossoming folk scene and the establishment met head-to-head in the park. 'For years weekend folk singing has been a tradition in Washington Square Park … But in the spring of 1961, the city rescinded its customary permit for singing in the park. This triggered a protest demonstration on April 9th… which was put down with excessive force by the NYPD.' A predominantly good-natured crowd of around 300 gathered in the square to protest the rescinding of the performing licence in what became known as the Beatnik Riots. Signs read: 'we shall have music' and protesters claimed that Commissioner Morris was suggesting that 'folk music brings degenerates and bad people. It's not so.' Protest leader Izzy Young, who had put up a handwritten notice in the window of his Folklore Center saying: 'Protest rally at the fountain', recalls that 300 gathered quickly 'without a telephone call'. As the day progressed and amidst the shouts of 'You're trying to kill the Village' and 'Citizens of America, we have a perfect right to sing', there is a lone cry: 'Real estate is at the bottom of this!' 'Got it in one!'

As much as the Beatnik Riot of 1961 was a clash of the growing '60s counterculture establishment, an attempt to stop the Swinging Sixties before it had got up any momentum, it was largely the latest chapter in a long running battle for the valuable eight acres in the midst of New York City.

Property developer Robert Moses had been attempting for many years to run a roadway through the park to connect Fifth Avenue with Manhattan. His motivation was pure greed, and he would again be pitted against the Beatnik community in 1964, when he refused to book the Beatles for the World's Fair.

Dylan wrote a song about the Beatnik Riot of 1961 and in 1963, as the battle continued, he was said to have written a song for the Joint Committee to Stop Lower Manhattan Expressway. Typed lyrics later came to light containing the song, 'Listen Robert Moses'. The song begins, 'Listen, Robert Moses, Listen if you can, It's about our neighborhood that you're trying to condemn.' The chorus kicks in as follows:

> Very early, Dylan found his way to the Folklore Center and throughout the years, it was to remain an important New York location for him.
>
> **Map ref. 8**

> We won't be moved Buddy, we won't be moved,
> We're fighting for our rights and we won't be moved,
> We're fighting for our rights from our heads to our shoes,
> We're fighting for our rights and we aren't going to lose.

If 'Listen Robert Moses' is indeed an early Dylan protest lyric, then it's probably fortuitous that it never ventured near to a guitar. 'Masters of War' it isn't.

On the 50th anniversary of the Beatnik Riot, Mayor Bloomberg issued a letter commemorating the importance of this event. Ironically, at the same time and in the continuing battle to keep the musical legacy of George Margolin alive, the Parks Department was attempting another public performance crackdown. This time was a little different. As Park Commissioner Adrian Benepe said in 2011, 'If Bob Dylan wanted to come and play there tomorrow, he could … Although he may have to move away from the fountain.'

One of the Leaders of the 1961 Riot was the legendary Israel 'Izzy' Young, who approached the whole day with sanguine sensibility. 'If we get everyone singing "The Star Spangled Banner",' he figured, 'they can't hit us on the head while we're doing that.'

Izzy Young had opened his Folklore Center in 1957 at 110 MacDougal Street, between Bleecker Street and West 3rd Street. Until it closed in 1973, it was a pivotal part of the Greenwich Village folk scene, described by Dylan friend and folksinger Eric Von Schmidt as both a 'meeting place and a booking agency'. One wall of the ten-foot/about 3 metres wide room was a community bulletin board. Of Izzy Young, Von Schmidt says he was 'loud, energetic, disorganised, petty, big hearted and totally dedicated to serving the cause of folk music and folk singers.'

Very early in New York, Dylan found his way to the Folklore Center and throughout the years, it was to remain an important New York location for him. Of his first visit, Jack Goddard in *The Village Voice* quotes Izzy remembering Dylan: 'picking up an autoharp, he began mumbling about some bloke named Captain Gray, people looked on in amazement as he began hopping around a bit. He was funny to watch and anybody with half an ear could tell he had a unique style.'.

Dylan wrote a song, 'Talkin' Folklore Center', which recalled his earlier arrival in New York and his encounter with the laissez-faire Greenwich Village:

> 'I got on a subway, I took a seat
> Got out on 42nd Street
> Met this fella named Dolores there
> He started rubbin' his hands through my hair
> I figured something was wrong, so I ran
> Through ten hot dog stands, four movie houses
>   and a couple of dancing studios to get back on
>   the train!'

Once the Folklore Center closed, Izzy moved to Stockholm. A return to Greenwich Village was recorded in 1989 for a short film, *Talking Folklore Center*. Although he bemoaned the demise of the old Greenwich Village 'freewheelin' bohemian cafes and artists, that period is gone.' But he feels there is still a buzzing atmosphere: 'Thank God the buildings are still low.'

As Izzy sits and reminisces for the film on the steps of the old Folklore Center, he is approached by the latest in a long line of Village Poets. The young man proceeds to tell Izzy: 'Dylan Thomas was a poet in the Village and Bob Dylan was a poet in the Village … If I don't make it, I'm changing my name to Dylan Dylan.'

Chapter 5
THE MUSIC INN
by Dina Regine

While much of the Greenwich Village '60s scene has faded, and lives in passed down memories and tales told by locals, the Music Inn still holds its own. Living and breathing in all its vintage glory, it's the one spot on 4th Street where time stands still. Filled with some of the most eclectic instruments from all over the world, the Music Inn is the kind of store that you walk into, and realize, that you really need an instrument that you didn't even know existed prior to entering! The two floors packed wall to wall, ceiling to floor with instruments in this tiny shop, look more like a museum than a store. Many of the vintage instruments are truly a work of art. Then there's the record collection of endless rarities. You look around the space and think to yourself, 'How is this all fitting in here?'

The Music Inn was founded in 1958 by Gerald Halpern at 169 West 4th Street, just a few doors down from where Bob Dylan would find his first downtown home a few years later at 161 West 4th Street, paying only $60 a month rent. It's rumored that same building, built in 1910, sold for $6 million back in 2015. Positively inflation.

Jeff Slatnick, who owns the Music Inn now, is one of the most unique characters you will ever meet. Musician, artist, poet, storyteller, instrument repair man and keeper of the flame on 4th Street just about sums Slatnick up. When you look in his eyes, you know this is a man that loves what he does. He's passionate, and his enthusiasm about music and art is contagious. He's also old-school New York at its best. He first went to the Music Inn back in '67, and wound up working there for a short while before moving to California to study Indian classical music. He returned to New York to work at the shop in '76 and has been there ever since. Gerard Halpern left Slatnick the Inn when he passed in 2010, and it's still one of the few places in the West Village that looks just as it did decades ago – in a way, an unofficial landmark. It's also the go-to spot for musicians looking for authentic vintage world instruments, or for new sounds to incorporate

> The Music Inn, living and breathing in all its vintage glory, is the one spot on 4th Street where time stands still.
>
> **Map ref. 4**

into contemporary music. The discovery of new sounds can be very addicting for an artist. The Inn also sports a long list of celebrities who have shopped there.

I went over to the West Side to have a little chat with Slatnick, a man I've heard about, but hadn't met yet. I made my way downstairs to the lower level, and waited to speak to him while I found myself slowly falling in love with a vintage oversized, deep toned tambourine. The phones were ringing off the hook, with customers looking for all sorts of hard-to-find things, while random customers wandered in with questions about various instruments. There was also a sense of community at the shop; people just swing by to hang out and say hello. Something you don't see much these days, especially as all the mom-and-pop shops are being put out of business by massive corporate chains. I watched him juggle all his customers with a delightful calm and Zen, and waited for the perfect moment to introduce myself, and not keep him too long. I had a few questions I wanted to ask him, but once he started talking, it was a wonderful fast paced stream of consciousness. He was generous with the few memories he had of Bob Dylan.

'I first saw Bob singing at the Cafe Wha? with a girl (I think her name was Carolyn Hester). They sang this song "East Virginia Blues", and she sang the lead, and he sang the harmonies. I thought it was peculiar because usually the girl would be singing the higher harmonies with a guy singing the melody.' At this point Jeff sings part of the song to me off the top of his head, and for a moment I was transported back a few years. I asked Jeff about Dylan's purchases at the shop. 'He was a customer here, and he bought harmonicas, and harmonica holders back then.' He added: 'He came in and insisted his first record be put in the window ... we put it in the window'.

Jeff had a few more memories about his neighbor on 4th Street: 'Bob later moved into an office like apartment, a two bedroom on 12th Street, and continued to buy instruments from us. Then he moved up to Woodstock. One fond memory from his Woodstock days was when he came into the shop with Garth Hudson, and they were both looking at a Martin archtop guitar. They both wanted it. So I said to them, if they both wanted the guitar, I would get to decide who gets it. I chose Garth Hudson. Bob said, "Why?" I said, "'cause you get to be Bob Dylan ... that's enough!"' We both had a good laugh as Jeff recalled that moment. 'That was the last time I saw Bob. He later moved to California, and the rest is all history.'

Just prior to the pandemic and lockdown, the Music Inn was running a weekly open mic. The Golden Globe and Emmy winning series *The Marvelous Mrs. Maisel* cast the shop as itself for all the record store scenes. As of this writing, New York City is slowly getting back on its feet, and the Music Inn is still standing, and so is Jeff Slatnick. I think I'm going back to the shop to buy that tambourine.*

*Reader, she did!

Chapter 6
HOOTENANNY AT RIVERSIDE CHURCH

ootenanny is a strange word. A word that sounds like the tiebreaker in a spelling bee. For most of us it conjures up an image of a fun singalong, a joyous party that never ends. For Dylan these regular Greenwich Village jam sessions were all of this and more. For Dylan a hootenanny in a church was to be the place he met his muse and his mentor, where Dylan felt the romantic spark that would help to propel him out of that Village and on to a global stage.

Says the Old Troubadour John Winn:

Greenwich Village in 1960 was strangely welcoming, it did feel like a village ... I arrived on the same wave as Tom Paxton and Bob Dylan. Dave Van Ronk and Freddy Neil were prominent among those that had set the stage for the hordes of folk singing wannabes soon

> *to follow ... There were times when there were so many guitar pickers and banjo pickers stacked together on MacDougal Street between West 4th and Bleecker that it was like tryin' to walk through a field of brickleburs, you had to be mighty careful where you put down your feet so you didn't step on some young genius who was writing a new song that would change the world.*

Dylan had settled very well and very easily into life in Greenwich Village. He was soon becoming the life and soul of most gatherings and John Winn remembers well the bachelor party thrown by Noel Paul Stookey (one third of the folk trio Peter, Paul and Mary) at the Upper Westside apartment of Peter Yarrow (the second third). Most of the Village gentry had gathered, including Dave Van Ronk, Tom Paxton and the youthfully exuberant Dylan. Wine was flowing and Peter Yarrow was keen to keep the party noise down, to avoid annoying the neighbours. 'The lone bug in the rug,' says John Winn, 'was the young Bob Dylan.' Dylan was at the piano 'banging out his best imitation of Little Richard.' And 'the bug was that his energy on the piano was accompanied by a machine beat of his feet on the parquet floors.' Dylan would be persuaded to quiet down, but then the wine would flow and the beat would start up again. 'I looked over to see Peter on his hands and knees crawling

The Freewheelin' Bob Dylan cover launched countless tourist photo opportunities at the north end of Jones Street

Map ref. 3

underneath the piano trying to shove the Welcome mat from his front door underneath Bobby's feet between the beats.' Part way through the rockin' and a rollin' set, the impromptu muffler succeeded.

When Dylan finally hit commercial success, it was with his second studio album *The Freewheelin' Bob Dylan*. The iconic cover is a young Dylan arm in arm with the woman who was quite probably the most important player in his early New York history, Suze Rotolo. The image, taken by Don Hunstein, is as iconic an image as ever adorned an album cover: the picture that launched countless tourist photo opportunities at the north end of Jones Street, the corner of Jones and West 4th. A cultural image that vies with a zebra crossing in North London for the title of most famous middle of the road in popular music.

The image which forever stands as an enduring image of young love is, said Suze Rotolo, 'my identifier but not my identity'. The photoshoot for the album was, according to Suze, 'all very casual'. The original shoot was to be in their apartment for the album cover and showing Dylan with a guitar. But thankfully the apartment was too small, and they were cast out into a cold New York day with Dylan in a jacket 'not good for a New York winter' and Suze wearing every piece of clothing she could find. We see two young lovers in that album cover. Yet Suze said, 'I look at that picture with layers and I feel I look like an Italian sausage.' Ah, the stark reality of romance.

The Dylan jacket would pass into folklore – and, if a letter to the British fanzine *The Telegraph* is to be believed – physically in to the hands of a Dutch sailor named Rob Mori after Dylan lost a game of chess in a New York cafe. Surely a tale worthy of a song on the Dylan album *Blood On The Tracks*.

Suze Rotolo first saw Dylan at a Monday night Gerde's Hootenanny. As she revealed in *Rock Wives*, 'he played with a friend called Mark Spoelstra. And Mark Spoelstra had lovely shoulders.' However, Dylan had a secret weapon which would thankfully outdo Mark's lovely shoulders and thus change the course of music history. 'When I met Dylan, what I loved about him was the way he played the harmonica, he played with an earnestness that was wonderful.' Dylan was also to be smitten on meeting a woman who was would not only become one of the great loves of his life but who would also introduce him to so many cultural, literary and, since she was from a left-wing family, political influences. As Dylan writes in *Chronicles*, Suze was 'the most erotic thing I had ever seen'.

However, at Gerde's, they were merely ships that passed in the folk scene night.

Cupid's arrow would have to wait until 29 July 1961 and the somewhat unlikely venue of the Riverside Church.

What was billed as an afternoon of folk music was to be broadcast on the radio station WRVR. We know that Dylan performed the traditional songs 'Handsome Molly', 'Naomi Wise', 'Po' Lazarus' and 'Mean Old Railroad'. He also performed with Ramblin' Jack Elliott a send-up of teen music called 'Acne', written by Eric Von Schmidt.

According to Suze, 'Dylan took the stage mid afternoon and drew laughter for his protracted comic fumblings with a recalcitrant harmonica holder.' While comedy is not the first thing that would spring to mind when we now think of Bob Dylan live, Suze said 'when he started out as a performer he was playful, a combination of Woody Guthrie and Harpo Marx with a good dose of himself as a binding ingredient ... the audience was with him the moment he stepped on the stage. A sense of humor, however, was always his strong suit.'

There was also an impromptu jam session as recalled by John Winn: 'I had been at a New York City cocktail party a few days before said concert and was having a casual chit-chat with a manager type who had just returned from Japan. He was regaling me with how cheap it was to get hand-tailored garments made to order there. He referred to the suit he was wearing as an example and also mentioned that he was wearing monogrammed silk boxers shorts to match.' Very smart for 'a young feller from Hannibal, MO'. 'A few nights later, at the concert, Bobby, Suze, Ramblin' Jack and I were hanging out backstage. Jack had been telling Suze a hilarious story about cracks in the sidewalk and I told them the story about the cocktail party. I started singing an extemporaneous song about 'All the beautiful people in their underwear'. Bobby picked up his guitar and we started making up verses. Suze said the song lasted about half an hour. It was a hoot.' Sadly, the 30-minute song 'All the Beautiful People in Their Underwear' has yet to appear on a Dylan bootleg.

After the folk afternoon, the party continued at the apartment of Suze's mother and love blossomed. 'I really got to know Dylan more,' said Suze, 'we were kind of flirting with each other.'

Suze very quickly became not only Dylan's girlfriend but his mentor. Along with another Greenwich Village couple, Dave Van Ronk and Terri Thal, Suze and Dylan formed a formidable foursome. Suze met Terri at Terri and Dave's apartment on the top floor at 15th Street. 'After a few minutes, Terri walked from the kitchen wearing only a bra and panties. Her underwear was white cotton – nothing lacy or fancy or sexy about it – but that didn't make one bit of difference. At almost six feet tall, with the looks of a slightly off beat model, she made quite an impression. Her hair was dark brown, like her eyes, and she wore it very short accentuating her long neck. She had a low voice and spoke in a heavy New York accent with the vocabulary of a sailor.' This naval tendency was one of many ways the extraordinary Terri stood out in Greenwich Village. She was one of the powerful women whom Dylan relied on heavily at that time. Once, upstairs at the Gaslight, the men of the folk music scene were engaging in bawdy stories and lewd rhymes. Terri leaned over to Suze and whispered her own rhyme that included the line 'I once had a cunt 9 inches long'. Suze didn't like to let on that she had never heard this word before.

Terri recalls those times as a formidable four: 'Dave and I first met Bob Dylan in 1961, and we both thought he was a genius. We all became good friends and Bob spent a lot of time at our apartment. He thought I was smart … Dave taught him a lot about guitar, lectured him on left-wing politics and encouraged him to read Bertolt Brecht, the Goliard poets and François Villon. All satirical critics of their societies. Bob's fascination with these poets showed up later in his songwriting.'

'His girlfriend, Suze Rotolo, introduced him to theater and visual arts. The four of us roamed around the Village eating breakfast all day and playing poker in my kitchen in the evening.'

Terri was soon to take on a slightly different role, that of Bob Dylan's first manager. 'One day Bob asked me, "Would you get me gigs?" I said, "I'll try." I didn't even think of asking him to sign a management contract; we were friends.'

Terri took audition tapes to clubs in Springfield, Cambridge and Boston with only very limited success. Terri finally managed to persuade Lena Spencer who ran Caffè Lena in Saratoga Springs, a resort town to the north of New York City, to book Bob for the weekend. Lena, a manager in the style of Anthea Joseph at the

Troubadour Club in London, had founded the club in 1960 with her husband Bill with 'vague beatnik plans to make enough money from the venture for a while'. Bill left straightaway, and Lena kept going until she died in a fall in 1989. The Caffè Lena is still going as the 'oldest continuously running folk coffee house in the country'.

Dylan played there in July 1961. As Terri Thal recalls, 'Lena Spencer was always asking for acts to book. When I asked her to book Bob, she objected because he was too new and unknown. "Every time you need a new act at the last minute, I find one for you," I said. "Now I want a favor." Bob played there and bombed; the audience talked throughout his performance. At the end of the weekend, Lena called and told me never again to ask her to book Bob Dylan in the club.'

In the Village, though, Dylan's almost comedic folk routine was a hit. He was soon to attract the attention of a manager known to many as The Bear: Albert Grossman. Terri very graciously stepped aside.

Albert Grossman had been a part of the folk scene for some while, and he would be critical to Dylan's success. He had been trying to put together a group to replace the Weavers, who'd had an international hit with 'Goodnight Irene'. One of their singers was Pete Seeger, who had refused to testify at HUAC during the McCarthy era – enough in those days to halt a career.

Dave Van Ronk said of Grossman: 'Inscrutable would be the best way to describe Albert. His eyes had the look of the bottom of a Coke bottle.' Grossman would manage Dylan's career to the very top. It was a classic rock 'n' roll, manager and star relationship. As Dave Van Ronk astutely commented, 'Albert was easy to deal with. It wasn't until maybe two days after you would see Albert that you'd realize your underwear had been stolen.'

Chapter 7
PLACES TO STAY, 'CRUMMY' AND OTHERWISE

We have all slept in strange places. In 1978, when Dylan finally came back to London after a 12-year break, my sister and I slept on the rainy streets of Hammersmith to buy tickets. We will never know the first bed, sofa or floor that Bob Dylan slept on that night of 24 January 1961. What we do know is that, for the next few years, there would be a heck of a lot of them.

Indeed, it seems that the young folksinger slept on every bed and sofa in Greenwich Village in the early '60s.

One of the most significant sofas was at the McKenzie house. In 1965, looking back at this time, Dylan recalled, 'Eve and Mac McKenzie, they really took me in and they were beautiful. They took me in and I lived with them. And they fed me and it was on 28th Street. And I stayed out all hours and came in and went to sleep on the couch.' The McKenzies' son, Peter, was a good friend to Dylan and remembers his couch time fondly:

In mid-May 1961, when I was 15 and a sophomore in high school, an eager, slightly disheveled but clean 19-year-old Dylan showed up at my parent's doorstep in New York City. He was supposed to stay just one night; when he finally did leave in mid-September, he had become an earnest adult. That was due in great measure to the personal guidance ... discussions about world history, politics, religion and other subjects my parents engaged in with him. What occurred during that stay is the unknown missing piece which makes up a key foundation for life decisions. People have been trying to figure out for generations why he forged the path the way he did.

Eve knew, over 60 years ago, what Dylan wanted. 'I want to be as big as Harry Belafonte, Eve,' he told her. He succeeded.

Woody Guthrie would spend weekends with Bob and Sidsel Gleason and so, therefore, did young Dylan. Sidsel, known as 'Sid', describes their young lodger: 'his hair in those days was long and curly and he wore that dark Eton cap. He had a pair of boots that were two sizes too big; everything that child had was either too small or too big. He bought a jacket, for instance, that didn't fit him at all and I think he paid seventy-five cents for it in one of those Village thrift shops…'

'He was just living here and there and everywhere in those months. I used to ask, "Bobby, would you like to take a bath?" He needed a bath. That child needed a bath.'

Dylan would lay his head down wherever he could, and he would write wherever gave him an opportunity. Chip Monck lived in the basement apartment at the Village Gate. Dylan 'spied the IBM Selectric (typewriter). He typed while I worked at The Gate. That gave him like six hours, he'd just drift in, I gave him a key and he'd sit down and type and then I'd come back in and he'd go, or we'd have a drink or something. We really never spoke much.' In that room, Dylan wrote 'Hard Rain' and 'Ballad of Hollis Brown', typed on the IBM. 'All the crumpled-up sheets in the basket,' said Chip, 'I ironed out and took back to the Hamptons and put underneath the barn.' When Chip returned they were gone.

As was the New York way, Dylan also took up residence in hotels, which by and large, ran as cheaper and slightly more temporary accommodation. The most famous of these is the Chelsea Hotel. Situated in Manhattan and located at 222 West 23rd Street, between 7th and 8th Avenues, it launched a thousand careers – and almost as many books about the rooms.

Spencer Leigh in his book *Bob Dylan: Outlaw Blues* describes the Chelsea Hotel as 'being built in 1884, it was the tallest building in New York. Although not the most luxurious of hotels it still became a home for artists, musicians and writers including O. Henry, Thomas Wolfe, Aaron Copland, Willem de Kooning and Arthur C. Clarke. Bob Dylan was to write 'Sad-Eyed Lady of the Lowlands' there and Leonard Cohen wrote about a fling with Janis Joplin in 'Chelsea Hotel, #2'.

The most immediate Dylan reference comes from the song 'Sara' on the album *Desire*, in which Dylan tells us, with remarkably unusual insight, that he was 'staying up for days in the Chelsea Hotel, writin' "Sad-Eyed Lady of the Lowlands" for you.'

In 2018, when the hotel was being renovated, the doors to many of the rooms, each of which told a tale, were auctioned. The room where Leonard Cohen had an affair with Janis Joplin, as well as Joni Mitchell (different time), went for $85,000. Jimi Hendrix's door went for $13,000. The door to the room shared by Andy Warhol and Edie Sedgwick, a couple described in *Vanity Fair* as 'Romeo and Juliet with kink', went for $52,500. The door to the room where Jack Kerouac wrote *On the Road* sold for $30,000. The biggest prize was the Dylan room, Room 211, which sold for a remarkable $100,000. All the more remarkable since Dylan led a very quiet life there. As biographer Howard Sounes commented, 'he had a piano in his room and he composed songs but few people knew he was there.'

On Friday, 28 August 1964 perhaps the most iconic meeting in popular music took place at a New York hotel, the Delmonico at 502 Park Avenue.

The Beatles had just played at Forest Hills Tennis Stadium and their meeting with Dylan was brokered by journalist Al Aronowitz. The meeting is best known for the myth that Dylan introduced the Beatles to marijuana. However, in his 2014 *Guardian* article 'When Dylan met the Beatles – history in a handshake?', Andrew Harrison makes a far more important cultural point. 'It's Sherlock meets the X-Men, it's England meets America, it's Dylan's adopted dustbowl past meeting the Beatles' democratised hyper-pop future, one side nourishing the other'.

* * *

The Joan Baez song 'Diamonds and Rust' contains the line 'that crummy hotel, over Washington Square'. That hotel was the Hotel Earle, in 1986 renamed as the Washington Square Hotel. On the hotel's official website, they say, 'Yep, folks, we were that crummy hotel over Washington Square – and damn proud of it, truth be told, the place *was* falling apart all those years ago, before the Paul family purchased it in 1973 and remodeled it.'

The Hotel Earle situated at 103 Waverly Place alongside Washington Square Park, was built in 1908 as a small eight-storey residential hotel. It became popular and kept growing, nine storeys by 1910 and a further three added in 1917. In April 1918, Ernest Hemingway arrived in Greenwich Village and stayed there for three weeks prior to serving in the First World War as an ambulance driver.

As was often the case, by staying at the Hotel Earle, Bob was following in the footsteps of the other Dylan, Dylan Thomas. In the 1950s, Dylan Thomas and wife Caitlin were evicted from the Beekman Hotel and found a room, described in a letter to his parents as 'right in Washington Square, a beautiful Square, which is right in the middle of Greenwich Village, the artists' quarter of New York.' Their other reason for moving, which Dylan Thomas neglects to mention, is that it was staggering distance from a favoured watering hole, the Minetta Tavern.

By the 1950s Village Preservation magazine told us, 'the hotel's sophistication had fallen, so the atmosphere became more laid back, room prices dropped and the bohemians started to come around.' By the time the other Dylan checked in, the hotel was well on the way to 'crummy'. Bob first rented a room prior to his first major gig at Gerde's. His stay cost him $19 a week – not cheap then!

Dylan stayed in Room 305, and it was here that pretty much all of his relationship with Joan Baez took place. Joan gives a good reason for largely staying at the Hotel Earle with him – 'yeah, he was a 20-year-old guy and you didn't go to a 20-year-old guy's apartment 'cause they were nasty.' Despite opting for 'crummy' instead of even worse, Baez has fond and romantic memories of their time there. Later she told *Rolling Stone* that in winter, 'we were staying at the Earle in the Village. We were leaning out of the window one morning watching the kids. I felt as if I had been with Bobby for a hundred years, and all the kids wandering around out there were our own children, you know? This couple looked up and I know they recognized us. They were beautiful…'

At one stage Dylan, Peter La Farge and Ramblin' Jack Elliott all lived on the third floor. One day Ramblin' Jack came back to find Peter La Farge in a bad way and his 'whole bed was covered in blood. He had been stabbed working security for someone shady and been stabbed in the chest several times. He refused to go to hospital!' They all survived the third floor to, by and large, not tell the tales.

In 2020 letters that Dylan sent to a Minneapolis coffee house scene friend, Tony Glover, went to auction. The letters were from 20 January, 1962. In the address section Dylan had crossed out 'Book of the Month Club' and written 'Bob Dylan; Hotel Earle; New York.' He wrote: 'Back now in that city and thinking of all that whistling harmonica music you are making back there in that dungeon hole … We went one time to see John Lee Hooker paying his dues to the blues at Folky City … If you wanna write me – send a letter to Bob Dylan – Earle Hotel – Washington Square North – New York, NY. That's about all for now I guess - I'm starting to play poker sometimes to pass my worries away – I got about 25 dollars worth of worries now.'

He concludes the letter by quoting Woody Guthrie – 'This world is yours, take it easy but take it, Woody Guthrie.' Then he adds a postscript – 'My girlfriend says that you don't sign your full name to friends so … Me, Bob.'

Chapter 8
A STAY AT WASHINGTON SQUARE HOTEL
by Bret Johnson

It is hard to overstate our enthusiasm for the Washington Square Hotel. So many New York hotels tend toward Williams Sonoma opulence and corporate sterility – '80s business grays and someone else's creepy idea of luxury. This is a family hotel and it shows. The Washington Square can feel like a patchwork of compromises that don't quite satisfy or unify. But that's its charm, the sort of messy compacts that only make sense in a family. Here the joy is in the quirk: the décor's quirky, eclectic, sometimes kitschy, but offset by the unexpected. The common areas are festooned with a warmth of baubles and hidden ceramic mosaics, peculiar decorative flourishes and sometimes gauche afterthoughts – I love it.

There's so much talk about boutique hotels, and in the city these tend to be overpriced and unfeeling. They're the sort of hotels that try desperately hard to stand out, to be green, to be vintage, to seize on whatever luxurious fad has seized us; they try to trick us into an 'experience.' But they all ring false, and worse, they trust us to participate in our own betrayal. Especially the ones that capitalize on their own historicity. Not so with the Washington Square Hotel. It's neither fake nor starchy. If anything, it's humanely American. It's one of the few family-owned hotels left in the city, and the owners are everywhere, lovingly attentive.

It is personal. That is the heart of its appeal. This is a deeply personal hotel. And Dylan is nothing if not personal. Here you can request Dylan's old room, 305, where he stayed for a spell in '64 (yes, made famous by Joan Baez). Don't look for any grandness. The layout of this floor remains largely unaltered, and his room looks out not onto the park but into a shaftway – if Dylan had stuck his arm out the window and reached, he could probably have slapped the brick wall on the opposite side. But I love this. The hotel doesn't bend over backwards to sell you on this room. It's just a room – an affordable room. Next door, 306, Peter La Farge's room sits empty. Snatch it up. Sing 'Ira Hayes' in the dark. Pop down the hall and you'll find Ramblin' Jack's room at 312 (it's now a suite, if you're feeling fancy). To stay in these rooms is at the very least to inhabit the precise square footage, bounded by the same walls, the same windows, as their previous occupants. Open the curtains and turn off all the lights. Now stand and breathe deep, in and out, full deep breaths. Wait for your eyes to adjust, stare out your window at the brick wall across the shaft. You may no longer find the Village peopled by a fury of young artists creating themselves before your eyes in bursts of wonder, but if you listen closely you can just make out the echo of chatter, a thrumming guitar and a song in the distance.

With refreshing persistence, the hotel cultivates its relationship with the Village, participating in its culture and advocating for the neighborhood in its endless tug-of-war with NYU's ever-expanding ambitions. The hotel's owners genuinely care about preserving the Village as a living place for future generations. They're founding sponsors of the Village Trip, an annual festival at Washington Square Park that celebrates the musical traditions of Greenwich Village. Every Sunday they host a jazz brunch. On the weekends their Village Nights lure performers into the bar space for an intimate musical evening, open to the public, and frequented by locals as much as hotel guests. Some nights the locals will outnumber the guests. This is a hotel that rejoices in its neighborhood milieu. And that is the joy of staying at the Washington Square Hotel. As a guest you are not confined to a bubble of tourists. You are enmeshed in the life blood of the Village. The water pressure, I'm told, is excellent.

Chapter 9
TWO DYLANS AT THE WHITE HORSE TAVERN

At times I have been known to down three small tots of Heaven's Door whiskey to help me through a sitting of the Dylan film *Renaldo and Clara*. The legend of the White Horse Tavern is built on a rather more tragic feat of drinking. A legend so shrouded in mystery that even in the confines of this very book there are two different versions!

One of the many Greenwich Village mother hens who provided a roof, clothing and support to Dylan in his early days was Mikki Isaacson. When she first met Dylan, she recalled her reaction to being told his name. 'I remember the first time I asked him how to spell Dylan. Like in Dylan Thomas? I said. No, he replied, like Bob Dylan.' Whatever the origin of the name change from Robert Zimmerman – and the Welsh poet is a pretty prime candidate for the source – in New York

Bob Dylan often followed in Thomas' steps. Following a path that took him to The White Horse Tavern.

The White Horse Tavern has been described in lyrical terms by the Dylan (Bob) writer David Hajdu: 'A smoky pub on Hudson Street where young literary hopefuls congregated because they had heard that Dylan Thomas had dropped dead on his way out of the front door in 1953 … The White Horse could generally be counted upon to provide at least one writer who drank and any number of drinkers who wrote.'

Dylan Thomas was a White Horse Tavern regular, although in both New York and London I am still searching for that elusive bar which has a plaque that says: 'Dylan Thomas never drank here'. The White Horse Tavern is nevertheless the real deal. There is a photograph of him standing at the bar, staring at the camera and daring the viewer to join him. Framed, it hangs in the bar. And he's still staring, still daring.

Legend has it that a doctor told him that one shot of whisky would kill him. So he took himself off to the White Horse Tavern, where it took 18 shots before he finally keeled over and died. Other versions of this tale are available.

In the 1960s the White Horse Tavern was still a hard-drinking, carousing bar which tended to resound with the hearty melodies of a celtic nature. It was Greenwich Village Party Central. As Suze Rotolo recalled, it was where she was 'introduced to the paralyzing effect of Irish whiskey'.

The Clancy Brothers were regular performers there, and Liam Clancy was acutely aware that something very special was happening in Greenwich Village in the early 1960s. In John Bauldie's book *Wanted Man* Liam said: 'It was a certain sort of spontaneous combustion. It's a thing that happens around the world at different times. It happened in Paris in the Twenties when Hemingway was writing: a mini Rennaisance. It moves from place to place, and there are people who try to find out where it's going to happen next, to follow it. But you can't control it, you can't predict it. What was happening at the Village at that time – it was a surprise to find yourself in the middle of it.'

Bob Dylan had not only found himself in the middle of it but had rapidly pushed himself to itse very centre. 'He was a teenager,' recalled Liam Clancy 'and the only thing I can compare him with was blotting paper. He soaked everything up. He had this immense curiosity. He was totally blank and was ready to suck up everything that came within his range'.

The songs of rebellion that often shook the White Horse Tavern spoke to Dylan louder than love or life or death. Writer Sean Wilentz commented that Dylan wanted to 'change over songs to make them fit an American landscape.' What Dylan heard from the Clancy Brothers and others night after night at the White

Horse Tavern inspired Dylan to go to the New York Public Library. There he read stories of the American Civil War from publications such as the *Pennsylvania Freeman*. As Dylan said, 'you become aware of nothing but a culture of feeling, of black days, of schism, evil for evil, the common destiny of the human being getting thrown off course.' Dylan saw that a very specific creative path was being shown to him. 'Back there, America was put on the cross, died and was resurrected. There was nothing synthetic about it. The godawful truth of that would be the all-encompassing template behind everything I would write.'

For Dylan the music that he heard at the White Horse Tavern was an inspiration, an education and an increasingly clearer creative path. Dylan achieved this while all around him was whisky and carousing.

> The Washington Square Hotel is where you can request Dylan's old room, #305 where he stayed for a spell in 1964.
>
> **Map ref. 5**

When Liam Clancy saw Dylan at the Newport Folk Festival in 1965, he could detect the fruits of a White Horse Tavern education. When Dylan broke in to 'Mr Tambourine Man', Clancy recalled in 2002, 'I found myself standing there with tears streaming down my face because I saw the butterfly emerging from the caterpillar! When he sang: "My ancient streets too dead for dreaming", I knew it was Sullivan Street on a Sunday.

So it was not only a street, it was our street. I suddenly realized that this kid who had bugged us so often, had emerged into a very major artist.'

Dylan's apartment at 161 West 4th Street

Showing the way to West 4th Street

West 4th Street at Jones

The Music Inn, 169 West 4th Street

The Freewheelin' Bob Dylan cover location, Jones Street at West 4th Street

Directing you to Bleecker Street and MacDougal Street

Dylan's 1970s townhouse at 94 MacDougal Street

GREENWICH VILLAGE LOCATIONS

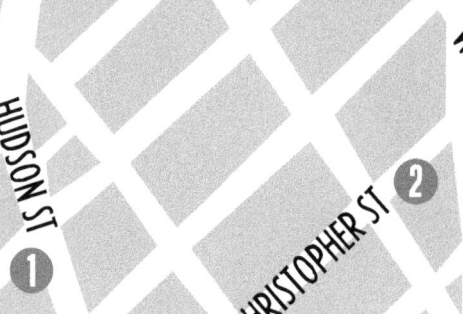

1. WHITE HORSE TAVERN, 567 HUDSON STREET
2. KETTLE OF FISH (ALSO FORMER SITE OF LION'S HEAD BAR), 59 CHRISTOPHER STREET
3. THE FREEWHEELIN' BOB DYLAN COVER, NORTH END OF JONES STREET AT WEST 4TH
4. THE MUSIC INN, 169 WEST 4TH STREET
5. WASHINGTON SQUARE HOTEL (FORMERLY HOTEL EARLE), 103 WAVERLY PLACE
6. GASLIGHT CAFE, 116 MACDOUGAL STREET
7. CAFE WHA?, 115 MACDOUGAL STREET
8. FOLKLORE CENTER, 110 MACDOUGAL STREET
9. ORIGINAL SITE OF KETTLE OF FISH, 114 MACDOUGAL STREET
10. DYLAN'S TOWNHOUSE IN THE 1970S, 94 MACDOUGAL STREET
11. THE BITTER END/OTHER END, 147 BLEECKER STREET
12. GERDE'S FOLK CITY, 11 WEST 4TH STREET

MacDougal Street and the Minetta Tavern Restaurant

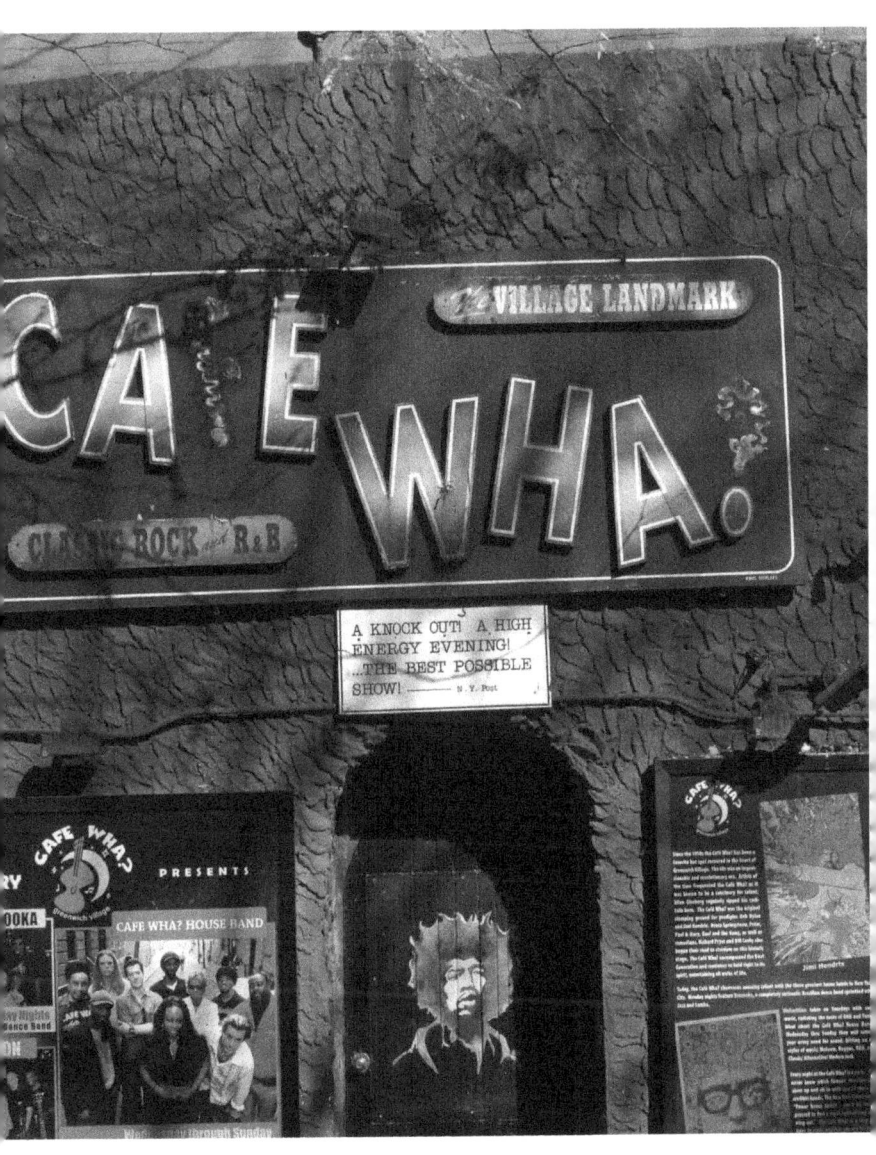

The famous Cafe Wha? on 115 MacDougal Street

Washington Square Hotel (formerly Hotel Earle), 103 Waverly Place

Washington Square Park and Arch

White Horse Tavern by day!, 567 Hudson Street

White Horse Tavern by night!, 567 Hudson Street

The Beacon Theater (amazing ceiling) at 2124 Broadway (at West 74th Street)

Chapter 10
IN 'THE OFFICE' AT THE KETTLE OF FISH

Normally if a little local bar is the venue for a historic meeting, they will put up a picture, a plaque, sometimes rename a section of the bar. I was lucky enough to co-curate a whole room at the Troubadour in London to commemorate the appearance of Dylan there in 1962. The Kettle of Fish, though, hasn't been the site of just one cultural, musical or historic meeting; it has been the site of three.

There has been a Kettle of Fish bar in Greenwich Village since the 1950s. Jack Kerouac was pictured 'well refreshed' standing by its neon BAR sign. It was originally at 116 MacDougal Street and has moved twice, now being situated on Christopher Street just off Sheridan Square. The neon sign has moved with it but is now located inside and out of the New York winter chill.

At its original site in the early 1960s, it was upstairs from the basement venue, the Gaslight, and as Suze Rotolo recalled, 'it lacked only the bar flies and liquor license necessary to accommodate them.'

The Kettle of Fish soon became known as 'the Office', a useful hangout for the Magnificent Four of Bob, Suze, Dave and Terri.

Suze said that one day Dylan burst in waving a piece of paper: 'Hey, you gotta listen to this song I just wrote, but maybe I just heard it somewhere.'

The Kettle of Fish became the backdrop to many critical episodes in Bob Dylan's early career and right through the 1960s.

In 1965 Dylan married Sara Lownds, but the marriage was kept secret for a long time. In November 1965, Ramblin' Jack Elliott came upon Bob and Sara at the Kettle of Fish, 'Congratulations, Bob!' 'For what?' replied Bob. 'I heard you got married.' 'I didn't get married.' 'Well, I'll be darned! I swear I heard that you got married! I heard from two people that you got married!' 'No, I didn't get married,' Dylan assured him: 'If I got married, you'd be the first person, I'd tell.' He had. Jack wasn't.

In the Kettle of Fish, Dylan would meet three figures who would be important to his career – Jimi Hendrix, Edie Sedgwick and Leonard Cohen.

Dylan had watched Hendrix play at the Gaslight. Dylan's comment was somewhat obvious: 'Incredible.' They moved on to a local bar (and Dylan magnet), the Kettle of Fish. Dylan did not say much apparently, as we would possibly expect. Hendrix biographer David Henderson recalls the scene and the mutual respect: 'the best testimonial was sitting in the Kettle of Fish in full view through the wide windows that looked out on narrow MacDougal Street, getting drunk and laughing a lot. That was the highest endorsement.'

Dylan told Hendrix of the time he had met the jazz pianist Thelonious Monk. 'When Dylan introduced himself by saying he played folk music on MacDougal Street, Monk had replied, "We all play folk music."

Edie Sedgwick is said to be the woman on whose head balanced a 'Leopard Skin Pillbox Hat', the debutante in 'Stuck Inside of Mobile with the Memphis Blues Again' and the blonde who is the muse to *Blonde on Blonde* and beyond.

And her meeting with Dylan was also at the Kettle of Fish. As Bob Neuwirth, a constant Dylan companion, recalled, Dylan and entourage 'occasionally ventured into the poppy nightlife world' and someone had said to Dylan 'you have to meet this terrific girl'. Dylan called her and sent a limousine to collect her. There was only one place to meet. A place that Bob Neuwirth described as 'one of the great places of the sixties', the Kettle of Fish.

That meeting began one of the iconic '60s *ménages à trois*, a threesome of love/hate and every emotion in between. A complex passion, a volatile triumvirate of Bob, Edie and her future mentor, Andy Warhol.

Edie's biographer, Jean Stein, stated that Edie 'believed that to sit around was to rot. An extension of the sixties pop culture from a Bob Dylan song, "he's not busy being born, is busy dying".'

Stein quoted from one of Edie's friends Heide, describing a later Kettle of Fish meeting which encapsulates vividly the tempestuous relationship of this trio: 'When I got there, I saw Edie. She had tears in her eyes. I asked her what was wrong. "I try to get close to him [Warhol], but I can't."' Warhol arrived and nothing was said. 'We were all just sitting there when a limo pulled up to the front door. Bob Dylan walked in. Edie perked up, began talking in her little-girl Marilyn Monroe voice. Nobody else spoke. It was very tense. According to Heide Dylan grabbed Edie by the arm and he said 'let's split'.

The third iconic meeting at the Kettle of Fish was a meeting of two of the finest songwriters the planet has ever seen – Bob Dylan and Leonard Cohen.

Cohen's biographer, Leil Leibovitz, sets the scene for that first meeting: 'curious about the young Canadian singer, Dylan summoned Cohen to the Kettle of Fish, the MacDougal Street joint where he spent many evenings drinking. No record survives but it is reasonable to assume that pleasantries were uttered and exchanged.'

The meeting was after Cohen had performed at the Bitter End and Dylan had the manager, Paul Colby, bring him to the Kettle of Fish.

There is a second Dylan/Cohen meeting, often cited as taking place in 1970 in the dressing room after Cohen had appeared at Forest Hills Tennis Club in Queens. It is said that Dylan turned up unannounced to see him and wasn't recognised and when told that Dylan was there to see him, Cohen had replied 'So?' This seems somewhat implausible unless all the admiration had worn off after just one year.

Cohen describes Dylan in 1988 as a 'Picasso – that exuberance, range and assimilation of the whole history of music.' Dylan's praise of Cohen is a little more, well, 'Dylanesque': Cohen, he says, is one of the few people he wouldn't mind being. Interestingly the other two picks are Roy Acuff, the cowboy folksinger, and Walter Matthau, the curmudgeonly actor.

Chapter 11
HORSE AND KETTLE – DYLAN'S VILLAGE BARS
by Bret Johnson

I can't promise you'll find Bob Dylan in a bar, any more than I can promise you will find him in the Grand Canyon at sundown. Nor can I swear by sojourns such as those recommended in these pages. I can't confidently speak to what nostalgia accomplishes. But in a city so regularly ravaged by change, that seems to hold nothing precious, I do believe there remains some salvageable heart of the Village, of the old Village, to unearth and explore and treasure.

Few storied bars from Dylan's day remain with us. It's a tricky game pursuing the ones that do and not always worth the effort.

The Kettle of Fish has changed locations three times since the '60s. From the original MacDougal location (now a Vietnamese restaurant) to West 3rd Street (where it replaced Gerde's, already enjoying its second incarnation) to their present address at 59 Christopher Street, a couple doors down from the Stonewall Inn. But don't let the Kettle's history of relocation and reinvention dissuade you from paying them a visit. Few bars in the city have undergone so much change yet retained their essential appeal.

There's no mystique nor spell that made the original Kettle special. Perched above the Gaslight on MacDougal, where was better for Dylan than the Kettle to celebrate a gig or to loosen up before one? Convenience may have lured Dylan up the stairs, just as it did Kerouac and Corso and Ginsberg before him, but for Bob the Kettle became a kind of private institution, more clubhouse than 'office.'

> The songs of rebellion that often shook the White Horse Tavern spoke to Dylan louder than love or life or death.
> **Map ref. 1**

Here Dylan could speak in confidence or preen, escape into naked laughter, or disappear behind his shades. Something rarer than mere expedience kept him and his cohort returning long after fame opened the city to them: something unpretentious and familiar, an intimacy in the atmosphere that blends with the noise of a drunken fight but is not diminished by it. It was the kind of bar you want to call home. And it still is.

Today's Kettle of Fish is the rare tavern to retain not only the feel of its golden era, but also a mixture of its past with a fuzzy anticipation of the needs of the present, of us, of now. The afternoon crowd is local, and generous with a tale; in the evenings there's a smattering of everybody: bridge-and-tunnel, tourists, Villagers, NYU kids rallying, thirtysomethings falling in love, reminiscing retirees, pen-clutching poets wandering in to sip bourbon amidst the shades of fallen legend. If the Packers are playing you'll likely find a huddle of five crowding the lone TV, their muted cheers blurred by the juke box riffing overhead. The brick walls ache with a warmth that cannot be faked. Manhattan's as much washout as gem, and an equitable bar is hard to find, where the spirits are affordable and the beer's cheap, especially these days. We need places that celebrate anonymity: with corners to hide away in for stolen kisses or quiet conversation, yet also with open spaces to lounge and preen and celebrate. The Kettle seems to effortlessly invite stranger and regular alike into a fine camaraderie, an egalitarian city night.

For the Dylanologist, today's Kettle has added perks. Across the street lies Christopher Street Park. If you remember your Suze Rotolo, you'll know that she took Dylan to the newspaper stand on 7th Avenue South, at the west end of the park, to pick up Robert Shelton's 1961 love letter to Dylan, reviewing his performance at Gerde's in the *Times*.

While you're there, pause to take it in. Little in scale or surface has changed about Christopher Street Park in the last 60 years. Enjoy it!

Also worth noting: until 1996, a few years before the Kettle took up house, 59 Christopher was the Lion's Head, famed haunt to some of the city's best journalists of the '60s. So many were the writers gathered here, that it became tradition to hang their dust jackets on the walls in dizzying collage. To hear the old-timers tell it, it can seem like everybody who ever lived in the Village drank here. The Clancy Brothers were late-night regulars, wandering in after some uptown gig, instruments in tow. By closing time you'd find the whole bar on their feet in song, lamenting young love in a roaring Irish brogue. Pete Hamill, who you might best remember for authoring the liner notes to *Blood on the Tracks*, preserves the spirit of the Head in its prime with typical pathos in *A Drinking Life*. Pick up a copy.

During the Stonewall Riots in June '69, while the regulars at the Lion's Head sat at the window and sipped their pints, Dave Van Ronk walked over to investigate. A veteran of anti-war and civil rights demonstrations, he instantly threw himself into the melee, got knocked out by the cops and arrested. As Van Ronk later recalled, 'Anybody who'd stand against the cops was alright with me and that's why I stayed in.' It's worth mentioning not just because of Van Ronk's significance to the Village folk scene and in Dylan's youth, nor just because it's a cracking anecdote, but because the Lion's

Head, whatever else it may have been, was also an Irish working-class bar of its generation. The loveliness is in the change. It's 2021 and we can romanticize these old places, but let's share a little gratitude that their attendant cruelties are fading.

On a recent spring evening I sat out front of the Kettle with Adrienne, one of the owners. You can feel her spirited engagement in everything: moving through the crowd like a yogi, wine in hand, missing nothing, barking laughter, her voice equal parts rasp and throat. I had the feeling of visiting a troubled friend I'd loved when young, whom I'd taken for lost – only to discover her as alive and vibrant as I remembered, that the death drive of youth had been milled into thoughtfulness. Adrienne and I watched a gathering of LGBTQ youth, giddy after the long isolation of lockdown, a huge smile on her face as she turned to me. 'This is great. This is so great. In the old days this never would've happened'. She read the question on my face. 'Too Irish. Too old school. But this, this is great, this is how it should be'

> The Kettle of Fish became the backdrop to many critical episodes in Bob Dylan's early career and right through the 1960s.
>
> **Map ref. 2.**

Whereas the Kettle of Fish sustains its spirited allure, today the White Horse Tavern is no more than a glossy caricature of its golden days. Though the White

Horse looks much the same, nothing about it evokes the spirit of its history – ironic for a bar that makes so much of its own past. There are photos on the wall, ballooned to monstrous proportions. The menu even quotes Dylan Thomas! How much more authentic can you get? But the burgers are $20 a go, $14 for a cup of soup. It feels more like a tacky hotel bar than a special experience – and if you want to drink at a hotel bar, just stay at your hotel bar.

Among the oldest continuously run bars in the city, the White Horse opened in 1880 and for a lovely mid-century moment was famous for its spot in the literary zeitgeist. Dylan Thomas, of course, collapsed on his walk home after 18 shots of bourbon (or 31 or 23, the numbers change depending on the source). Here, too, the Clancy Brothers made themselves regular four-players in the back room. Anaïs Nin, James Baldwin, Norman Mailer (on Sunday afternoons) all held court, boozed and brawled. Kerouac's alcoholic antics remain a ballyhooed point of pride. And, of course, Bob Dylan – of course.

The White Horse may still be an institution but precisely whose I can't say. There's precious little to appreciate in visiting it in 2021, aside from enjoying a peek at the interior, which remains largely unchanged. I cannot promise it will be true in another year or five. The building was acquired back in 2019 by one of the city's more notorious slumlords. An avaricious developer – here unnamed, though you're encouraged to dig deeper – he has a record that suggests a man indifferent to nostalgia and contemptuous of romance. If you found Bob Dylan at the White Horse in 2021, I suspect you'd wish you hadn't.

If you are visiting the White Horse, or find yourself in that stretch of the West Village, you'd be better off slaking your thirst across the street at WXOU Radio Bar, at 558 Hudson Street. Enjoy a cheap drink with twice the bonhomie. WXOU has been around since the '80s, and where gentrification has obscured so much else in this neighborhood, here the feel remains much unchanged. The drinks are cheap, the setting close and intimate, the music excellent. Show up on a Wednesday afternoon and, much like at the Kettle, you're more likely to meet Villagers who knew Dave Van Ronk, or Suze Rotolo, or who have a ready Steve Earle anecdote to share, than you will ever find at the White Horse Tavern, that expensive mausoleum to hip and faded culture.

Chapter 12
TALKIN' TROUBADOUR TALES
with Terri Thal

Terri Thal was Bob Dylan's first manager and a Greenwich Village friend and mentor. She was and is a New York legend:

'At first sight, I thought Bob had a touch of genius. I've never been able to articulate precisely why. When I met him, he still was playing primarily the music of Woody Guthrie. He seemed to be an inept performer, stumbling around on stage, but I quickly realized that his stage presence was reminiscent of Charlie Chaplin's, and had a purpose – getting the audience to be on his side. As he incorporated a wider variety of songs into his repertoire, and as he started to write songs, he stopped trying to sound like anyone else and that very distinctive singing style emerged.

We spent many evenings together. Dave Van Ronk, Suze Rotolo, me – and Bob. I met Bob before he met

Suze. As they became a couple, our topics of conversation didn't change substantially. Dave and I talked a lot about social change, as we did with all of our friends, even if they weren't interested in it. Dave and I considered ourselves Marxists and were members of a socialist organization. We tried to get Bob – and other friends – to understand that the problems they read about, such as poverty, war, and racism weren't individual, separate issues but were related parts of an overall system. Like our other folksinger friends, Bob never became interested in deep, systemic change.

Suze came from a left-wing family; her mother had been a communist, but when we met Suze, although she had a perspective that was well to the left of Bob's, she didn't talk about it much … most of the political proselytizing came from Dave and me. At that time, Suze still was quite young; her concern about social issues increased as she got a bit older.

Of course, we talked about folk music – Dave and I were interested in its relationship to the culture that created it – how the songs reflected aspects of society. I had taken a seminar in American Studies in my last year of college, taught by a brilliant historian, and we had delved into the relationships among events, the culture that produced them, including music, visual art, and literature. I found it fascinating to look at where a folk song came from and how it fit into its cultural background. Dave was interested in anthropology and cultural change.

There also was whatever talk occurs among fairly young adults, and a lot of penny poker. Bob wouldn't – and at that time, probably couldn't – put up a larger stake in the game, and we were playing for fun, not money, so that was OK with Dave and me.

Bob frequently sang new songs he'd arranged or written for us, including those with a social justice thrust, but he didn't talk much about any interest in political lyrics. Even then, he seemed to be moving beyond that to music with a wider appeal. He certainly resisted all attempts by Dave or me to get him to become more political.

I wasn't surprised that Bob asked me to be his manager. He wanted and needed to work, but couldn't book himself – especially outside of New York City. There were few managers for young folksingers, and we were friends. Working with me was a very sensible thing for him to do, and we had an unofficial arrangement; we had no written agreement, and I didn't ask for any money for the few jobs I booked him into – I said I'd wait until I was getting him work more steadily.

If Albert or another more commercially-oriented manager come along and hadn't offered to manage Bob, I would have continued to do so. I expected more clubs to open in nearby areas and, as they developed audiences, I thought I would be able to get him more gigs and, eventually, a recording contract. When Albert offered to manage Bob, of course Albert didn't talk to me first – you don't ask permission of another manager to take away her client, and he wouldn't have known about Bob's arrangement with me unless Bob told him about it, which I'm sure Bob didn't do. Bob didn't talk with me about it until after he had agreed to work with Albert. Yes, I was hurt, but I recognized that as Albert booked Peter, Paul and Mary or other more commercial acts, he'd be able to book Bob into the same rooms or concert halls; and Albert certainly was more able to pull the strings that opened up engagements for his performers than I was. So I simply congratulated Bob and we continued to be friends.

Eventually, Bob moved into another social milieu.

Chapter 13
LAUGHTER AND FIGHTING ON ELIZABETH STREET

The whole world waited with baited breath throughout the latter part of the 1960s for the first Dylan novel, *Tarantula*. I waited in my own South London corner of the Dylan world. When it was eventually published in 1971, this world had no idea of the wrestling that had been going on in Dylan's mind, in the offices of the publishers Macmillan & Scribner, let alone the very literal wrestling that had taken place on the pavement on Elizabeth Street.

In the summer of 1969, Dylan moved back with the family to Greenwich Village – to, as Anthony Scaduto describes it, 'a duplex in a townhouse he bought on MacDougal Street just a shuffle away from the old scenes, near the Gaslight, Kettle of Fish, Bitter End, Gerde's.'

Terri Thal says that Dylan was looking for a piece of his past: 'he disappeared up to Woodstock, cut himself off and now he seemed to be looking to find what he'd been missing in the music world. The music, plus actually looking to catch up with his past.' Look to his past but just to see a way to move forward. 'When he visited me,' says Terri, 'he looked at his old corduroy cap, which he had given me. He said he wanted to see it. I held it and he looked at it and he said, "Wow, what a great cap." I asked, "Would you like to hold it, take it?" And he said, "No, I don't want it." He just wouldn't touch it.'

Dylan had become aware of a potential private oasis in the very midst of the beautiful mayhem of Greenwich Village. A community of 21 terraced homes with 11 lining MacDougal Street and 10 running parallel on Sullivan Street. 'Between them,' the *New York Times* tells us, 'is a large interior courtyard shaded by an English style hedgerow. … It's a secret garden in the middle of the city, hidden from the streets.' Among the many famous residents over the years have been Richard Gere, Baz Luhrmann and Anna Wintour, whose daughter Bee Schaffer commented, 'You could go across the garden to your friend's house in a way that's so rare in New York.'

It was called 'The Garden' by residents, created in 1921 'as a co-operative community for middle class professionals looking to escape the larger apartment blocks.' Ironically, those who were unable to escape the Bleecker Street and Houston Street apartments could, according to the official history, 'look down longingly into "The Garden"'.

In this idyllic rural retreat in the midst of New York, there were fireflies in the summer. And on moving in, one friend commented that Dylan's 'biggest worry was where to send the kids to school'. It would transpire that this was far from Dylan's biggest worry in moving to 94 MacDougal Street. In a rather ominous portent for the chapter in Dylan's life that was to unfold, The Garden was the inspiration for the set of the Alfred Hitchcock film *Rear Window*.

Alan Jules 'A.J.' Weberman was and is a Bob Dylan fan. He was first turned on to Dylan's music as a student at Michigan State University. He recounted in *Rolling Stone* in 1971, 'I liked his music, his songs were political. They'd talk about the things that mattered at the time. You dig me? He was singing about the problems of black people and the poor. Nobody was singing those songs the way Dylan was and he totally turned me on.'

A.J., as many fans have always done and always will, spent a lot of time listening to Dylan's lyrics. 'I realized it was poetry and required interpretation. I developed the Dylanological Method, which is looking at each word in the context in which it appears and looking for words that have a similar theme that cluster around it (concordance). I started to devote a lot of time to just sitting around interpreting Dylan's poetry.' However, A.J. took his interest a step or several hundred further.

He felt that his hero had taken a wrong turn and it was for A.J. to point this out. He developed his Current Bag (CB) Theory. 'Once upon a time Bob Dylan walked the earth, a revolutionary prince with a guitar on his back, he loved poor people, black people and the disinherited. He was a regular John Wesley Harding. Then came the CB, the CB enslaved our free-spirited hero and turned him into a quiet, fear-filled little man who lives with his family on MacDougal Street afraid of political contact (*Rolling Stone*, 4 March 1971).'

A.J. began to root through the Dylan family garbage for clues that might support his theories. He found pet food, baby nappies, but the world's first self-styled 'garbageologist' also found a manuscript to Dylan's novel *Tarantula*. A.J.'s publication of bootleg copies forced Dylan to finally publish, despite his own misgivings. A.J. continued his garbage quest, to be confronted by Dylan's private secretary, Naomi Saltzman: 'Don't you have anything better to do with your time?' A.J. replied, 'No, no it's a really good thing. There's going to be an article about it in the newspaper *East Village Other*.'

A.J. set up the Dylan Liberation Front, whose office would answer the phone with, 'Dylan Liberation Front, we mean business.' To help with assessing Dylan's current health status, an advert was placed in the *Village East Other*: 'If anyone has a sample of Dylan's urine, please send it to me c/o Evo East 12th Street, New York.'

Things very much came to a head when Dylan and A.J. came to blows during a confrontation on Elizabeth

Street, an incident which A.J. touches upon in his interview which follows this chapter.

On 23 May 1971, when Dylan and family were in Israel, the Dylan Liberation Front decided to hold an anti-birthday party. One of their members, David Peel, armed himself with a cowbell, drumstick and police whistle, and gathered a crowd in Washington Square Park, a crowd which soon swelled to over 300. The crowd were told, 'We're going to Dylan's house now, it's the rich house next to the Hip Bagel. You know why it's the Hip Bagel? Because Dylan made a pretzel out of you...'

The anti-birthday party, complete with its own cake, continued in loud, but thankfully law-abiding, fashion for some while until one of Dylan's friends, Al Aronowitz, successfully broke the crowd up a little by announcing, 'Free hot dogs down the block that way.'

By December 1971, Dylan had bought a property in Malibu and moved the family out. A.J. still lives in New York. In the song, 'Where Are You Tonight? (Journey Through Dark Heat)', Dylan talks about 'laughter down on Elizabeth Street'. One assumes that Dylan couldn't find a suitable rhyme for the phrase 'unseemly scuffle'.

Chapter 14
A.J. WEBERMAN SPEAKS

March 29, 2021

A.J. starts our conversation by referring to early Dylan as 'before I spaced him out', but all these years later and still viewed as 'the bad guy', A.J. remains very much a Bob Dylan fan.

'I first started listening at Michigan State University. I would lift up my dogs' ears and sing "Freight Train Blues" to them.' A.J. views Dylan as 'the poet laureate of American literature, not just of rock 'n' roll. Guy's a fucking genius. It's all there, man. He is a genius beyond comprehension.' Beyond comprehension to all but A.J. Weberman. 'Academics who study Dylan's lyrics are way off the mark. You have to have lived through it. You have to have a knowledge of the folk scene. You can't just be a college professor. You have to know the guy.' He gets the lyrics about 'heating pipes just cough' from 'Visions of Johanna'. You have to know the layout of Gerde's in a loft, the plumbing of the Gaslight.

Although A.J. views Dylan's descriptions of his early life as 'smoke coming out of a boxcar door', he views Dylan's autobiography *Chronicles* as 'pretty accurate'. He has researched the stories. He has traced the potentially fabricated characters such as Ray Gooch.

A.J. has no regrets about the anti-birthday party of his garbology. He does regret the day he confronted Dylan's wife Sara at the house. It was after the Concert for Bangladesh, and he started yelling at Sara, 'If the garbage means so much to you, why do you throw it out?' He deeply regrets this: 'You don't fuck with someone's wife. I shouldn't have been disrespectful. I should have headed for the hills.' In the aftermath of this confrontation came the infamous fight with Dylan in Elizabeth Street. During their scuffle, Dylan tore off A.J.'s Bob Dylan button and threw it to the ground. As they scuffled, 'bowery bums came up and asked, "Hey, man, did you get much money?" "No, that's Bob Dylan!"' As Dylan rode off on a bicycle, A.J. picked up a bottle and took aim. 'I could have hit him, knocked him into traffic. I had a good arm from all those riots.' A.J. relented: 'sometimes you just got to take your licks.'

Years later A.J. was watching the video to 'Duquesne Whistle'. As Dylan throws something out of the car window, 'That's it!' exclaimed A.J.. 'That's my Bob Dylan button!'

Still a Dylan fan, A.J. feels he shouldn't be seen as 'the bad guy when I revived his fucking career!' At the time of the album *John Wesley Harding*, 'Dylan told me, "A.J., before you came along, the records were just sitting on the shelves!"'

A.J. says he still listens 'to all his stuff. I don't read into [it] though. I extrapolate.' From the album *Rough and Rowdy Ways* (2020), A.J. listens to the track 'False Prophet' and says, 'Yeah, that's absolutely Dylan.' On the other hand, he listens to a track like 'Idiot Wind' (from 1974) and says, 'Yeah, that is definitely me.' A.J. can watch Dylan give a speech at Musicares and say: 'Some people were harder to pin down' and reply: 'That was me, that was a glorious moment.' Is A.J. a Dylan fan after all this? 'I love the guy!'

Chapter 15
NEW BEGINNING AT THE BITTER END AND BOB AT THE RESERVATION

Most of us have a comfortable place in the world, to where we return again and again. A place that we view as home. For me that was and is South London. For Dylan it was and is the creative melting pot of New York.

In 1975, Dylan bounced back to New York like the proverbial rubber ball. He would spend most evenings drinking Mouton Cadet with Ramblin' Jack Elliot and Bobby Neuwirth. And the centre of Dylan's world at this time was a cafe called the Other End and its club, the Bitter End. The Bitter End changed it's name to The Other End in 1975 and changed it back a few years later.

Dylan had hung out here before. He said in 1962 that 'sometimes I go for about two weeks without making up a song ... I wrote about five songs last night, but I gave all the papers away. It was in a place called The Bitter End.' The building on Bleecker Street had, according to Robert Shelton, been a 'cheerless bistro which had floundered financially.' Owner Fred Weintraub had converted it to the Bitter End. Its enterprising manger, Paul Colby, saw the possibilities of launching a Greenwich Village Folk Revival and launched the latest in a long line of folk festivals as the First Annual Village Folk Festival. As he noted: 'Hyperbole was always standard advertising procedure in the Festival.' Dylan made an appearance. On his return in 1975, Colby gave Dylan a booth at which he could hold court. It was from this booth that Dylan devised the album *Desire* and gathered together the motley crew that would embark upon the Rolling Thunder Revue. It was where Dylan plotted his new beginning.

At the time, as Jacques Levy explained, Dylan had 'no real plans ... to do anything.' Dylan told him, 'I really like the stuff you do with Roger McGuinn. How about you and I do something together? 'Which was slightly strange right? Because he knew I did lyrics, and I knew he did lyrics. But I said I'd give it a shot.'

Despite the unlikely collaboration, this worked perfectly well for Dylan and Levy. After one of those many apocryphal chance meetings on a New York street, Dylan went back to Levy's apartment. He sang 'One

More Cup of Coffee' and 'Sara'. Returning to the Other End, Dylan wrote out the lyrics to 'Isis'. As Levy recalled, 'Everyone sat there, glued.' Their collaboration, and the set of musicians who gravitated to the booth at the Bitter End, was inspired. Dylan's wife Sara had returned to New York to see if there was 'some kind of getting back together'. But it was the meeting of the two other women in the same week in June 1975 that were to prove pivotal to Dylan over the coming years.

The meeting with the violinist, Scarlet Rivera, is documented in her own words in the chapter that follows. The other, Patti Smith, was at the time an inspiring singer and Dylan had come to see her band. Patti, who was a huge Dylan fan 'like when you have a crush on a guy in high school', told the tale to Jimmy Fallon on *The Tonight Show* in 2020:

> *He came to see our band ... when we were making some headway in New York ... and then he came backstage and back in those days Bob was scarcely seen. And I loved him so much. But he came in the room and he says, 'Hey, is there any poets in here?' and I said, 'I hate poetry.' I acted like a jerk. I don't know what came over me, like a teenager, like Sixteen Candles. You know when you like the boy, but you don't want the boy to know you like him. They took our picture, and it was on The Village Voice. And I was so embarrassed. I thought, 'Oh, he's going to think I tried to exploit him.' I thought he would be really mad, but I was walking down the street in the Village and here he*

comes. And he had the newspaper with him, and he said 'Uh, do you know these people?' I looked at him and I said, 'You're not mad?' And he said 'No.'

Patti described their meeting as 'tarantula meets mustang'.

The Village Voice of 2 November, 2016 beautifully describes a meeting of these two at the Bitter End and during the Rollin' Thunder Revue rehearsals: 'She asked if she could get up with the band. Amused at this seemingly frail waif, Dylan said yes … they huddled onstage, looking for a song they both knew and settling on "Money", Barrett Strong's Motown classic. Bob sang backup, Patti sang lead, and man, you could hear that she knew the subject matter – which things are free, and which things cost, and how you could get lost between those poles. Her heart was up there in her throat, where it's been ever since.'

The collaboration with Jacques Levy and the musicians who ventured to the booth at the Bitter End was eventually to produce one of Dylan's biggest commercial and critical successes, the album *Desire*. However, the sessions at the CBS Studios on 52nd Street did not begin well. So many musicians had been assembled that another studio had to be converted to a green room to accommodate them all. There was a constantly running buffet for musicians and their entourage. Among the musicians were Kokomo, the English jazz funk band. Rob Stoner, who was eventually brought in as a session leader, says that 'Kokomo was too large an ensemble for what was being attempted at the *Desire* sessions. They also seemed inexperienced in the delicate art of accompanying a performer embodying the subtle dynamics of Bob Dylan's presentation.' It is fair to say that the sessions weren't harmonious on any sides. At one point, the producer Don DeVito shouted: 'OK, guys, that's the end. Bobby's lost his voice.' 'What fucking voice?' retorted the Kokomo guitarist Jim Mullen.

Rob Stoner was an inspired choice to bring order to the chaos.

In his early career, Stoner had played the same folk clubs as Dylan with Rockin' Rob and The Rebels, a reflection of how public taste was shifting away from acoustic acts. Stoner had been a fan of Dylan's 'since his early days, especially after he stopped imitating Guthrie'. Greenwich Village had been a vital stepping off point as well as a source of critical income, just as it had been for Dylan a decade or so earlier. Doner says, 'My involvement in the Village folk scene was only as a source of employment, hired as musical accompaniment for various artists. Living a few blocks from the folk clubs and being able to sing and play their material on a variety of instruments without rehearsal, gave me an edge over other sidemen.' Versatility never goes out of fashion in the Village.

Desire was a platinum-selling album in many countries, including the US, the UK and the Netherlands.

It was a wonderful return for Dylan. As ever with Dylan, fine tracks were left off the album. This time, 'Abandoned Love' was to become a kind of cult classic, with one outtake in the public domain and only one ever performance at the Bitter End.

Fan Joe Kivak recalls that night. 'On a Tuesday night in July 1975, I headed out to see Ramblin' Jack Elliott at the Bitter End in New York City ... I glanced around the club and was stunned to see Dylan seated toward the back with Jack, wearing the same striped t-shirt and leather jacket he had on in a photo with Patti Smith on the cover of the then current *Village Voice*.' As Dylan sang this new song, 'everyone in the room was in a triangle ... it was an incredible feeling to be in that small club listening to Bob Dylan perform a new song.'

Although many view the only studio outtake as a superior version, one that includes an exquisite violin from Scarlet Rivera and uncredited vocal harmony from Rob Stoner, that one and only performance at the Bitter End on 3 July 1975, will forever remain in Dylan folklore.

On 22 October 1975, at an appearance of David Blue, and over the following nights, Dylan sat in his private booth at the Bitter End, putting together a tour. The tour that Scarlet Rivera described as 'a mythical carnival that came to life', the Rolling Thunder Revue.

Dylan already had the core of his roving troubadours from the *Desire* sessions, such as Rob Stoner and

Scarlet Rivera. He toyed with some of his old Greenwich Village compadres, but Phil Ochs, who was to die of cancer five months later, and Eric Anderson didn't make the cut. The beat poets Allen Ginsberg, Peter Orlovsky and Anne Waldman did join the circus.

Dylan added an extraordinary line-up of musicians who auditioned at the Bitter End booth: Mick Ronson, one of David Bowie's Spiders from Mars; T Bone Burnett; and the talented multi-instrumentalist David Mansfield, who was still in his teens and had been a member of the band Quacky Duck and his Barnyard Friends. The singer from *Desire*, Emmylou Harris, dropped off the scene to be replaced by Ronee Blakley, who Dylan met at the David Blue show.

> In the summer of 1969, Dylan with his family, moved back to a townhouse in Greenwich Village.
> **Map ref. 10**

The Rolling Thunder Revue, which has been documented in all its mystical glory in book, film and albums, was a tour unlike any other in musical history. Allen Ginsberg has said that the dominant theme for the tour was 'respect for mother goddess, eternal woman, earth woman principles.' It was significant that were powerful cameos from significant women in Dylan's story, including Joan Baez, Scarlet Rivera, Joni Mitchell and Patti Smith, who turned down the opportunity to join when her former boyfriend Sam Shepherd signed up to document the tour.

One of the most memorable and mystical moments on the tour happened when the circus stopped in New York state. One of the tour excursions had taken place in a Native American sunrise ceremony. Around a campfire, members of the tour took part in a campfire ceremony as 'an affirmation, a renewal, the generosity of the Great Spirit. Members of the tour took it in turns to voice their hopes.' Peter Orlovsky said, 'I pray that we should all eat well and stop smoking cigarettes that are bad for us.' Dylan nods.

Ramblin' Jack chips in, 'May the spirit of this tour extend to everyone we meet along the road.'

When it is Dylan's turn with, as road manager Larry Sloman said, 'a Tibetan scarf flowing in the wind,' he gives hope and says, 'I pray that man will soon realize that we are all of one soul.' It's a thought that underpins much of Dylan's music.

On 16 November 1975, Chief Arnold Hewitt at the Tuscarora Nation Reservation has a phone call asking if the Rolling Thunder troupe could drop in for a visit. It was a request that was granted and a visit that was outlined by both Martin Scorsese in his film of the tour and Mad Bear, who is seen greeting Dylan. The visit was at the Community House, which sadly is no longer there. As Mad Bear outlined, 'a few of the younger Indian children played tag around the Community House' while the audience 'feasted on corn soup, corn bread and venison.'

The song that Dylan chose to sing that day was a powerful ballad, which continued Dylan's tradition of recording social justice and whose writer was a link to Dylan's early days in Greenwich Village. 'The Ballad of Ira Hayes' was the tale of a Pima Indian who had fought at the Battle of Iwo Jima in the Pacific Islands. The photograph by Joe Rosenthal of the US Marines raising the Stars and Stripes became a powerful symbol of America in the Second World War. Marine Corporal Ira Hayes, in the words of the song, 'returned a hero, celebrated throughout the Land/he was wined and speeched an honored/Everybody shook his hand.' Only weeks after attending a ceremony for the Marines with Richard Nixon in 1954, Ira Hayes was dead at the age of 32 of alcohol and exposure, lying face down in a ditch. 'Call him drunken Ira Hayes, he won't answer anymore … not the whiskey drinking Indian, nor the Marine who went to war.'

Dylan recorded the song. As did Johnny Cash, who recorded a whole album of pro Native American songs. The writer of this ballad was Peter La Farge. Described by Dylan biographer Anthony Scaduto as 'part Indian, cowboy, folksinger, author of Ballad of Ira Hayes, weaver of tall tales', La Farge, like Dylan, had spun his own mythology in the early '60s folk scene of Greenwich Village. He was not, as sometimes cited, a Pima Indian but was part French and part Narragansett

Indian. Apparently, though, even that last bit is up for debate. His father Oliver had won a Pulitzer Prize in 1930 for his novel *Laughing Boy*, which had given a rare, positive view of Navajo youth.

Dylan has sung the praises of Peter La Farge on the notes of the 1985 album *Biograph* – 'actually Peter is one of the unsung heroes of the day. His style was just a bit too erratic. But it wasn't his fault. He was always hurting and having to overcome it ...We were pretty tight for a while. We had the same girlfriend. When I think of a guitar poet or a protest singer, I always think of Peter.'

Scaduto wrote that La Farge had ridden into Greenwich Village just slightly ahead of Dylan. When a young and naïve Dylan arrived, one of the many mother hens, Sidsel Gleason, had asked 'the tough Indian' La Farge to keep an eye on Bob. 'Bob was scared to death of him. Pete would walk into a party where Bob was and stand with his arms crossed, not saying a word, just watching.' And Bobby called me [Sidsel] one day and said, "Mom, please get that Indian off my back..."'

Strange as it may seem to us, Dylan and La Farge did indeed share a girlfriend in those early years in Greenwich Village. According to writer John Bauldie, this girlfriend was 'Avril the dancer,' a 'dancer and actress who saw Dylan perform at a Gerde's Folk City Hootenany'. This may have been as early as mid February 1961.

Avril briefly lived with Dylan on East 4th Street, but then one day she turned up at the MacKenzie house on East 23rd Street for Sunday dinner: 'He's gone. He just picked himself up and left.' Dylan was just visiting family in Minnesota.

La Farge wrote the 'Avril Blues' song in January 1962. It is a song which contains the fabulous lines 'Be kind to squirrels, don't kick giraffes / Remember we had lots of laughs.'

> The song had Avril off to conquer the world:
> Listen little lady, going far away
> You won't be back tomorrow…
> Pass up the world kid
> Dance to other songs
> You weren't here long
> Go teach the Greeks how they should dance

The reality was likely somewhat less romantic. It's likely that Avril the dancer just returned home to the San Francisco Bay area.

The career of La Farge, as with so many fellow Greenwich Village travellers, went in the opposite direction to Dylan. After one album produced by John Hammond for Columbia Records in 1952, La Farge was dropped.

Although his mother would always tell people that La Farge died in his sleep, Liam Clancy told a different tale in 1984: 'Peter La Farge, he committed suicide in my bathtub. I had an apartment on Sullivan Street – Bob Dylan lived next door. Peter La Farge had married the girl and they had nowhere to live. I discovered that my then girlfriend had been two-timing me with Dylan, so I quit. And Peter and his wife moved into my old apartment … And he died in my bathtub.'

Singer Tom Russell recalled: 'Pete was one of the first of the new folk circle to be signed to a major label and the first to die and be forgotten.'

At the end of 1965, when La Farge died, and throughout 1966, many Greenwich Village contemporaries, such as Paul Clayton and Richard Farina, died. Dylan was moving onward and upward, leaving behind, as Liam Clancy recalled, 'frustrated dreams and visions.'

'Dylan had taken off as a star into the firmament, he was one of us and suddenly there he was. Dylan was what every one of us probably hoped to be, and we realized now that lightning had struck. It couldn't strike twice.'

Chapter 16
TALKIN' TROUBADOUR TALES
with Scarlet Rivera

The popular music soundtrack to the mid 1970s for many fans was not the electric guitar but the haunting sound of a violin. To me, Scarlet Rivera is as magical and mystical a figure as ever graced a stage. Dylan and Scarlet was a rare musical alignment.

Writer Michael Gray sets the scene for their meeting chance meeting on 30 June 1975: 'Manhattan is full of determined-looking, skinny limbed young women striding along carrying violins or saxophones, but they don't usually have hair three foot long swinging down behind them.'

A car stopped by this determined young woman. The woman was Scarlet Rivera. In the car was Bob Dylan. These are her New York thoughts:

'I was from a small midwestern town as interesting as Hibbing, which is why I wanted to get out. Bob

Dylan had escaped as had Ramblin' Jack Elliott before him.

So you bet I escaped! I felt like a wild horse whose spirit would die if I didn't get out. My parents had my life mapped for me. Catholic college, which they would pay for if I agreed to be bought off and live at home, continue music only as a hobby and marry a local yokel. This was a no go! I had nothing in common with school mates or cheerleader type girls who were conceited and shallow. I secretly saved up money from summer jobs and got a music scholarship to SIU. When my only like-minded friend, Kathy Farrell, picked me up to take off for college, my parents exclaimed: 'Don't come back!'

I think I was born an activist waiting to be activated, and Bob Dylan was the spark. I had a strong sense of what I believed was right and just and did not share my parents' values. I saw through what I considered hypocrisy and bigotry. I didn't go along with being spoon-fed what to believe and revolted inwardly even against believing in the Church early on. I always loved wildlife and animals. And when the nuns told me that the Church ordained that animals don't have souls, that was the end of Church for me. I also didn't dig seeing nuns stripped of real authority and dressed in black to the ground, just parroting what the powers that be told them to do and say.

One day in high school, I heard Bob's voice on the radio singing 'The Times They Are a-Changin'.' It was like drops of water to someone dying of thirst in the desert. I bought the album *Freewheelin'*. I felt like I had lived in an intellectual and socially conscience vacuum, so his words made a huge impact, even though there was no one to share it with. I loved 'Girl from the North Country' and 'One Too Many Mornings' and 'Don't Think Twice'. Also, songs such as 'With God On Our Side,' 'Only a Pawn In Their Game,' 'Blowin' in the Wind,' and 'A Hard Rain's a-Gonna Fall' would soon influence my thoughts on the Vietnam War and the Kent State massacre of students by the National Guard of our own government.

I was on a mission to break the violin into popular music. I used the phrase, 'Black Panthers of string players'.

I played in a group in New York City before I met Bob, called the Revolutionary Strike Ensemble. And it was out-there music, bordering Jazz Fusion Avant Garde. I was introduced to The Band by Leroy Jenkins, a black jazz violinist who I sought out to take some lessons with. He told me I didn't need lessons, but he opened some doors for me. He introduced me to Ornette Coleman, who was my first paying gig in New York.

Even though New York in the 1970s was a big, tough badass place for a young girl from the Midwest, Greenwich Village was more gentle and always charming ... a respite from the otherwise cold and unforgiving city. It was a place of fellow adventurers, hippy clothes, head shops, people playing chess on the streets, musicians, artists, freethinking spirits. I never saw a single homeless person on the streets, only a few Bowery bums and drunks, but wandering around at all hours felt more innocent and safe. SoHo was a place where artists had inexpensive lofts to paint, draw and make art, so there was quite a creative vibe in the Village. The music club scene and coffee houses were vibrant with live music of all kinds.

I was going to a rehearsal on June 30 1975 on 13th Street in the East Village off First Avenue. A car pulled up. I was not aware at first glance that it was genuinely Bob Dylan driving the car. But as he insisted on hearing me play and as the conversation continued, I knew an extraordinary experience was unfolding. If I had kept walking, I believe another situation would have unfolded for us to meet, as I believe we were meant to meet.

Even while I was in the moment recording with Bob on *Desire*, I had no idea he would decide I would be an integral part of the final album, as there were so many other, more experienced, top players in the room. I had already experienced much disappointment and I tried to hold back having a definite expectation. But when I went back for the session, when I walked into the room and I realized all the big crowd of players were gone, just leaving a small core group in the room … well I began to think something significant must have been decided in my favor.

I would also give Bob lots more credit for the monumental decision he made overnight to change horses midstream, scrap the big band sound which included Eric Clapton and Kokomo, and go with the small band sound instead. I rode the waves of what was put before me like a good surfer, and I didn't fall off the board. I rolled with what was unfolding and like the gun battle at the OK Corral, I was the gunslinger left standing in the Durango after the smoke lifted and the room was cleared of the other cowboys.

I don't expect a *Desire Part II*, though. As the magical elements that materialized for *Desire* … I didn't see recreating themselves. Also, Bob is known for moving on both in material and concept. And that includes different lineups of musicians and soloists. I think the fact that *Desire* didn't become a predictable *Part II* made it, and the Rolling Thunder Revue, even more special.

The Rolling Thunder Revue was a mythical carnival that came to life. I felt integral to it. Take a look at what the Rolling Thunder Band would have been if I wasn't there. It would have been a male-only band and the sound, a wall of guitars. I brought a totally different tonality in sound and vibration, adding a strong melodic lyricism to the sound of the Rolling Thunder Band. I was a strong female presence that was elevated front and centre by Bob himself.

I was surrounded by the magnitude of being part of an amazing experience every day of the tour. I continually mused how I went from Cinderella to being in the Court of the Crimson King every night with Joni Mitchell on top of it. Considering I had a rough time and plenty of disappointment in my young life just prior to that fateful day with destiny when Bob discovered me, I marvelled at what was happening to me, that I had amazingly become an important part of the most important tour of the decade. A tour that countless musicians and artists would have given a pot of gold to have been on. But no one could even buy their way on to that tour. So, the fact that fate put me there was and continues to be something I marvel at with tremendous gratitude.

> A collaboration in a booth at the Bitter End was eventually to produce one of Dylan's biggest commercial and critical successes, the album *Desire*.
> **Map ref. 11**

The Night Of The Hurricane at Madison Square Garden was a Who's Who of New York in the arena and [they] lined up to meet Bob after the show. The Garden was considered the World's most famous boxing arena; [it was] where in 1971, Muhammed Ali fought Joe Frazier as two undefeated heavyweight champions of the world. This was where, if Rubin Carter had not been framed for murder, he would have claimed his title of middleweight champion of the world.

So, it was with great pride that I stood on that stage and performed 'Hurricane', knowing the signature lines

I created, captured the rage of injustice in the US and Rubin's plight. Muhammed Ali and Coretta Scott King were both there to show their solidarity with Hurricane and to keep his story alive. There was extra fire and electricity in the Madison Square Garden show.

I sing on albums now and if I wasn't so withdrawn at the time, maybe I could have envisioned singing with Bob, but I was terrified even at the thought of singing at all at the time. It's remarkable that I could go on stage fearlessly as an instrumentalist, but I couldn't fathom the thought as a singer yet. One time, when we were alone in the dressing room, he asked what I thought about singing with him. I froze like a deer in the headlights, and I said I just couldn't. As he knew I barely talked, I think he only asked me out of kindness and to draw me out of the remote place he saw I was in.'

Chapter 17
THE GREATEST BAND YOU NEVER SAW

Dylan fans learn very early in life that if you expect Bob to do something, he is likely to disappoint you. We learn that the most likely thing that he will do is the thing that you never expect. Unless he doesn't. *That*'s a surprise.

Two national television appearances at New York studios give us two defining Dylan moments, 21 years apart. At the first, Dylan shocked the world when he didn't turn up. At the second, Dylan shocked the world when he did. Prior to the official release in May 1963, Columbia Records put their full marketing machine behind promoting Dylan's second album *The Freewheelin' Bob Dylan*, the album that was set to become the breakthrough global bestseller.

The most immediate way of promoting an artist – well, it certainly worked for the Beatles – was a spot on the popular *Ed Sullivan Show*. In 1963, the Ed Sullivan Theater was located at 1697–1699 Broadway between West 53rd and West 54th Street in Manhattan. A 13-storey brick building, it had been built by Arthur Hammerstein and was originally named in honour of his father, Oscar. The theater opened in November 1927 with a play called *The Golden Dawn*. One of the stars was a young Archie Leach, who later changed his name to Cary Grant. In 1950, it was converted into a television studio and renamed CBS-TV Studios, Studio 50. And it was this studio that was set to host the television debut of a young Bob Dylan on 12 May 1963.

Rehearsals for the TV appearance had gone well. Dylan was set to share the show with the likes of Topo Gigio, a comedy mouse – as would befit 1960s TV variety. Dylan, in typical fashion, didn't pick a lighthearted number that might sit easily alongside a comedy mouse. Of course, Dylan, on the very cusp of commercial success, is going to pick one of the most overly political songs planned for *Freewheelin'* and certainly the most potentially controversial: 'Talkin' John Birch Society Paranoid Blues'. It's a song in which Dylan characterizes the right-wing John Birch Society as sympathisers of Hitler. Early 1960s variety TV it wasn't. However, all went well at rehearsals. Clearly no one at first picked up on the potentially explosive lyrical content. Until, as Dylan recalls, there was 'a big huddle'. On realising what Dylan was about to sing on national TV to an audience of many millions, the TV producers asked if

Dylan could sing another song. Suze Rotolo relates that Dylan was 'in a fit'. It was suggested to Dylan that he might sing a Clancy Brothers song but, as Dylan commented 'it didn't make any sense to me to sing a Clancy Brothers song on nationwide TV at that time'. Given the Clancy Brothers' repertoire of Irish rebel songs, it maybe didn't make a lot of sense for the TV producers to suggest them as the more acceptable face of folk music!

Looking back in 1984, Dylan was still rather bemused by the whole affair. 'Well, I don't know why I walked off that show. I could have done something else, but we'd rehearsed that song so many times and everybody had heard it.'

Walking off *The Ed Sullivan Show* only weeks before *Freewheelin'* was due to be released could easily have been commercial suicide for Dylan. Columbia Records had already circulated 300 promotional copies to radio stations, and these had to be recalled because they included 'Talkin' John Birch Society Paranoid Blues'. In fact, if anything, the walkout enhanced Dylan's reputation as an artist of principle and the reworking of *Freewheelin'* may have somewhat improved the album. As well as 'Talkin' John Birch Society Paranoid Blues', Columbia Records took off 'Rambling, Gambling Willie', 'Rocks and Gravel' and 'Let Me Die in My Footsteps.' The replacement for 'Talkin' John Birch Society Paranoid Blues' included 'Girl from North Country' and 'Masters of War.' Not bad. And the rest, as they say, is musical history.

On 30 August 1993, the David Letterman Show moved into the old CBS TV building and Dylan was to play again in the building in November 1993. At this show Letterman began by saying: 'Welcome to New York, the city that's on probation.' Dylan played 'Forever Young'. Dylan was also the last musical guest on the *Late Show with David Letterman* on 19 May 2015. David Letterman introduced Dylan by revealing that he had told his son Harry that 'there are really only two things you need to know in life: you have to be nice to other people and that Bob Dylan is the greatest songwriter of modern times.' Fittingly Dylan brought this particular curtain down with a rendition of 'The Night We Called It a Day'.

However, it was in 1984 that perhaps the most magical and memorable of Dylan's TV appearances took place. One that took everyone, probably even Dylan himself, by surprise.

In 1984 David Letterman's show was in the NBC Studios, which is part of the iconic Rockefeller Plaza. It was to be the scene of the most dramatic live television since the Moon landing.

Dylan was in a very difficult place musically and it was one of those occasional times when we find him somewhat adrift and in need of direction. 1983 was the time of the *Infidels* album. Dylan had left the classic song 'Blind Willie McTell' off this album; his judgement was all over the place.

It is said that Dylan's children were very keen on the punk ethos of bands such as The Clash. Maybe Dylan saw a little of the 1966 vibe in them. (In London in 2005, he would pay them the compliment of singing their song 'London Calling'.)

Quiet possibly through his children, Dylan had become interested in an LA garage, post punk band called the Plugz. Dylan approached their drummer Carlos Quintana and bass player to rehearse/jam/see what happens. They brought along a guitarist named Jeffrey Poskin, who often played under the name Justin Jesting or (and primarily at this time) J J Holiday.

Dylan was very interested in how he could adapt his music to their raw, energised style. As Quintana recalled in 1990, 'I think Bob has always listened to other stuff. He is not one of those guys who lives in a time warp.' So, the three young punks, in an old VW Bug, drove to the Dylan estate in Point Dune and were set up in the guest house overlooking the ocean. J J Holiday says that once the boys were settled in, Dylan came down from the big house wearing a raincoat, rubber boots and swinging a walking stick. 'To me, he looked like he had just got off the fishing boat.' Dylan had a large dog with him and when the boys were told it was called Baby, they fell around laughing.

There was clearly some magic at the rehearsals. They played Clydie King duets but primarily the sessions were fairly chaotic. At one point, J J Holiday says Dylan ask the band to play one song 'with a stripper beat and add a marching band to it.'

There were even suggestions of a South American tour, Dylan telling J J Holiday, 'Well, this won't be a Bob Dylan tour, this will be more like just a band playing gigs.' As Quintana tells us, 'Originally it was all very vague. There was talk of going to Hawaii and doing a show there.'

Eventually the reality of what Dylan had planned was revealed. In normal circumstances, the Letterman show was with a house band. For one night only, the band destined to play with Dylan in front of a global audience would be three punks hastily thrown together.

As Quintana said, 'and then the Letterman show came out of nowhere really. I think it was about a week's notice … It didn't matter whether it was a week or a month because we didn't know what we were going to play until about a minute before we went on air! We'd rehearsed the night before, but the night before we went through so many fucking songs we didn't know! He'd just start strumming and we'd jump in and follow it … and it would end the same way – he'd just stop playing.'

Before they played, the band had to hang around waiting for Ron Wood's Fender Stratocaster to arrive for Dylan. They were due to perform after Liberace cooked an egg casserole. Just five minutes before they were due to go on, the band were pleading with Dylan's tour manager, Bill Graham. 'Jesus Christ, we're shitting bricks over here! Can you go in and ask Bob what songs we're going to do?' Graham replied, 'He's not sure yet!'

J J Holiday commented, 'You'd think he would go to a great deal of trouble to get it together for a major TV appearance like that, but he didn't care what happened. That's what's great about him, we just went on the David Letterman show and jammed.'

Grainy video of rehearsals shows a number of tunes rehearsed by the band. And then on live TV, said bass player Tony Marsico, 'Right before we started, Dylan whispered: "Let's do 'Sonny Boy'."' (The 1955 Sonny Boy Williamson song and possibly a Dylan joke about going on a chat show and not chatting, 'Don't Start Me Talking.'). Thankfully, this was a song the band had played before or else, as Marsico said, 'we would have been totally fucked.' So, the virtual TV curtain rose on Bob Dylan … and a band no one had seen before, a band that almost no Dylan fan at the time would recognise at all.

An unrehearsed punk band with no real notice of what they are going to play is likely to crash and burn on live TV.

Not a bit of it. Sounding like the New York Dolls on heat, Dylan with his young band gave an extraordinary performance.

The Dylan writers lined up to eulogise. Clinton Heylin said that he gave 'the freshest and most intense performance he had ever given on national TV'. John Bauldie said that Carlos Quintana was 'one of the best drummers to have played with Bob Dylan'. With regard to the peerless version of his classic 'Jokerman', Michael Gray says that it was 'recreated almost as an impassioned, howling anthem on the very edge of chaos, yet knowing and lither, snarlingly fey and postmodern.'

Then in the middle of the performance of 'Jokerman' there is high drama, live on national TV, when for the best part of a minute Dylan can't find the right harmonica. He paces up and down, stagehands are called and what do the band do? They play on. These are the guys you would have wanted on the *Titanic*! Quintana, on the drums, says, 'when he fumbled around for the harmonica, I was just able to keep tapping it out – a couple of verses, a chorus. It seemed like ten years! The cameraman got so bored he actually did a close up of me.' Eventually we got an exquisite harmonica solo as the band played on.

The backline technician at the centre of Harmonicagate has recently been identified as Henry Edwards. Having been instructed to set up a harmonica in D, he was told in the midst of this live show that it should be G. Henry fetched the right harmonica. 'It took about 20 seconds but seemed like a fucking lifetime!' Henry felt that was surely the end of his Dylan career – but astonishingly a month later he got the call to be the guitar tech on the European tour!

Of the performance, Michael Gray commented in *The Bob Dylan Encyclopaedia* that 'thanks more or less equally to the Plugz/Cruzados and Dylan, it was a transcendent mainstream television moment – made the more gloriously surreal when Letterman came on, looking like a lost Bible salesman at the end of the first number, clasping his hands and telling the musicians it had been "very nice!". Very nice!' At the end of the set Letterman joins them on stage and says 'did you have a good time?' Dylan 'yes we did.' Letterman 'any chance you can play every Thursday night?"

So, after their triumphant New York night surely Bob Dylan and the Plugz conquered the musical world? Sadly not.

It is one of the most extraordinary of all the Bob Dylan what-ifs that after that night, Dylan moved on and we were never again able to see this wonderful band. Carlos Quintana said that he was calling Dylan's office two or three times a day to see about touring. And they would say, 'We're not sure yet. Call back in an hour. This happened for a fucking week. I didn't sleep for a week.'

After that, the Plugz morphed into the Cruzados, a band who had limited success. As John Bauldie recalled in 1990, 'After one glorious night playing with Bob Dylan in front of millions of people, they ... went back to being an unknown band.' The band did tour with Fleetwood Mac and played at Farm Aid. As Marsico said, 'playing to a hundred thousand plus crowd at Farm

Aid and standing between Neil Young and Arlo Guthrie singing 'This Land Is Your Land' while the sun sets, Wow! Did I dream that?!'

Sadly, Quintana and Marsico are no longer with us and J J Holiday, as Jeffrey Poskin, works on film music. Of the Letterman experience, he says, 'I cherish this very lucky time I was able to spend at such a young age with such a great artist as Bob Dylan ... He was gracious to me at all times as a young guitarist ... and as a fledgling human being for that matter.'

After the call to Quintana never came, Dylan put together a very experienced and professional band which included Mick Taylor, guitarist at various times with the Rolling Stones, and Ian McLagan of the Faces. The English music press rather harshly dubbed them 'an English pub rock band'. For the rest of the '80s, Dylan teamed up with the likes of Tom Petty and the Heartbreakers and the Grateful Dead. One critic, commenting on the lack of energy and the lack of jamming with the latter, asked: 'Why hire the Grateful Dead and not let them be the Grateful Dead? If Bob wanted a punk band, I'm sure the Plugz were free.'

For one glorious night, we had a glimpse of where a Dylan with the same 1966 raw energy, and the dynamism and pure musical chemistry he had with the band, might possibly have gone.

Keith Richards once said, 'the title of World's Greatest Rock n' Roll Band doesn't belong to a single act, it tends to move from band to band on any given night'. For one magical night on 22 March 1984 in New York City, Carlos, Tony, J J and Bob were that band.

Chapter 18
BOB AT THE BEACON

Toward the end of his annual tours, Bob Dylan often performs several concerts at The Beacon Theatre on 2124 Broadway at West 74th Street. This was the case in 2014, 2017, 2018 and in 2019. Dylan first played there in October 1989 and it's the venue he most often returns to in New York. He seems to be very much at home at The Beacon.

The Beacon Theatre is an historic theater. Built in 1929, it was designed in the art deco style by the architect Walter Ahlschlager. It was renovated in 2009, a restoration that caused Paul Simon, a regular performer there over the years, to comment in the *New York Times* (2009): 'I've performed here many times and it was always fun but I was overwhelmed to see how beautiful it is now. It is a great house with a great vibe and it's funkiness matched the music in a way… but it's nicer to have clean seats.'

Over the years it has hosted all kind of events from the Tony Awards to the Tribeca Film Festival but is best known for the leading musical acts that have appeared. The 1975 itinerary, for example, includes Fleetwood Mac, Supertramp, 10cc and the Kinks.

Susan Blanchard Ryan is an award-winning actress, star of the hit film *Open Water*. She is one of the many thousands of Dylan fans who have enjoyed magical nights watching Bob Dylan perform at The Beacon:

'I saw him at The Beacon for the first time in December 1995. I remember he made some comments about being tired because he hadn't slept well the night before because he was so excited to play in New York city. He can be so earnest and dear sometimes; it can break your heart.

I went twice during Bob's 2005 Beacon run of shows. One night it was very windy and my date got a piece of glass blown into his eye. We tried to wait it out, thinking it was just dust but it wasn't and he had to go to the Emergency Room. I didn't go with him but went to the concert instead. I found out later that he was upset and horrified by this choice of mine. But hey, I'm a hockey player's daughter and if you don't have a broken bone poking through your flesh then I figure you can probably handle it yourself! My relationship with Bob lasted. My relationship with the guy did not. I am at peace with that'.

Like many Dylan fans making the Beacon pilgrimage, Susan had favorite pre- and post-watering holes. La Caridad was an old diner with a large menu of what New Yorkers call Chino-Latino food. It was where Susan says that she would 'fuel up before a Bob show'. Sadly, La Caridad has become a casualty of the pandemic and many Bob fans will miss it.

Just a few blocks from The Beacon is the Emerald Inn. 'It is a classic pub, some might call it a "dive bar",' says Susan. 'Wonderful after a Bob show. You get a good mix of people in there and the roadies often show up with good stories to tell. I've been going there since the '90s and it hasn't changed one bit.'

The last time Susan saw Bob at The Beacon was in December 2019 and she recalls that he was 'wonderful, full of life with a twinkle in his eye. He seemed to be having a blast performing. I get so emotional every time I see him perform and basically sob off and on the entire time. Everyone around me thinks I'm crazy but that's just the way it goes. Art is supposed to touch us and move us. And Bob destroys me. Oh, the life of a Bob Dylan fan!'

AFTERWORD
by Maureen Van Zandt

Maureen Van Zandt is a dancer, producer and actor based in New York, best known for her role in The Sopranos. *She is founder of the city's Renegade Theatre NYC and co-host of the Generation Gap Podcast. She is on the board of the charity www.teachrock.org (founded by her husband Steven) and sits on the board of other music organizations as well. She is a New York rock 'n' roll Muse – and a Bob Fan.*

I became a real Bob Fan when I discovered the *Bringing It All Back Home* album in 1965. I was absolutely enthralled by every track on it and to this day know all the lyrics to 'Subterranean Homesick Blues' and most of the others … and then came the brilliant *Highway 61 Revisited*. One of my most vivid memories was getting off the subway at West 4th Street after a trip from New Jersey on a beautiful hot summer day and hearing 'Like a Rolling Stone' blasting from a car radio. There I was, a young girl arriving in what we all knew was the mecca of cool – Greenwich Village – full of hopes and dreams and excitement, and to have that song welcome me instantly made me realize I was where I belonged. I'd always felt like a misfit, but looking around at long-haired beauties dressed like peacocks, walking past a myriad of legendary clubs/cafes and hearing that song told me I was home.

With my best friend I went to see Dylan at a venue in Newark, New Jersey somewhere around '65; I believe it was the Mosque Theater (sometimes called Symphony Hall). We were very enthusiastic young girls and did not want to sit still in our seats, so we ran up to the front of the stage. Security guards at that time had seen way too many news clips about girls running wild at Beatles' concerts and I suppose saw us as somehow dangerous, so they grabbed us and tried to drag us back to our seats. Bob stopped singing, told them to let us go, and had one of them set up chairs on the side of the stage so we could sit there. I thought it was the coolest thing ever.

I think, aside from London, New York City was the center for music in those early days. Everyone who wanted to play music, or just loved music, flocked there to be amongst kindred spirits, to frequent the hippest music clubs, to hang out at the cafes and on MacDougal Street, which was so crowded with young people cars could barely get through. It was an incredibly rich time for music, fashion, art, spirituality. Peace and love was real, Baby! Where else could you see an unknown Jimi Hendrix play the Cafe Wha? or see Dylan or Lenny Bruce show up at the Gaslight for an impromptu set?

I believe artists are attracted to New York City because it's always represented freedom to be different, to take risks, to explore all the many unique places this town has to offer.

Greenwich Village has always been a haven for artists and has a relaxed, bohemian vibe, an old-world beauty, and an artistic history that you feel on every street. It's like its own country.

The Village has changed over the years and a few of the legendary places have gone, but for me it's still the best *place* in the city. I walk down those streets and feel the presence of all those beautiful ghosts; I hear the music; I see the magnificent old buildings, many of them landmarks; I taste the colors and the spirit. That history can never be taken away.

7

FINAL WORD

Mell and Lilian Bailey lived with their family in a tiny apartment at 185 East 3rd Street. At one stage in the early 1960s, as with many New York families, their apartment housed an additional young folksinger who slept on the couch, where he listened and he learned and he grew.

In 1973, after moving out of his 94 MacDougal Street, Dylan repaid the Baileys' generosity by offering his upmarket garden apartment to them at a greatly reduced rent.

When the opening of the Bob Dylan Center Archive in Tulsa was announced for 2022, the curators celebrated with a recording that had not been previously released. With many, many treasures to choose from, they selected a hitherto unknown recording of 'Don't Think Twice, It's Alright', from the autumn of 1962 – and a tiny apartment on 185 East 3rd Street.

Dylan has travelled such a long way from those early days, but he is never really very far from those New York couches.

LIST OF PHOTOGRAPHS AND MAP

Dylan's apartment at 161 West 4th Street

Showing the way to West 4th Street

West 4th Street at Jones

The Music Inn, 169 West 4th Street

The Freewheelin' Bob Dylan cover location, Jones Street at West 4th Street

Directing you to Bleecker Street and MacDougal Street

Dylan's 1970s townhouse at 94 MacDougal Street

Map: Greenwich Village Locations

MacDougal Street and the Minetta Tavern Restaurant

The famous Cafe Wha? on 115 MacDougal Street

Washington Square Hotel (formerly Hotel Earle), 103 Waverly Place

Washington Square Park and Arch

White Horse Tavern by day!, 567 Hudson Street

White Horse Tavern by night!, 567 Hudson Street

The Beacon Theatre (amazing ceiling) at 2124 Broadway (at West 74th Street)

LOCATIONS LIST

Al Grossman's apartment*   4 Grammercy

The home of Dylan's manager Al Grossman. Dylan sat on the front stoop for the cover of *Highway 61 Revisited*.

Allan Block Sandal Shop   171 W 4th Street

Site of many an impromptu folk jam although Dave Van Ronk commented: 'God help you if you wanted to buy a pair of sandals!'.

Allen Ginsberg's apartment   206 E 7th Street

Often a stop-off for Dylan in the early Village days.

Almanac House   130 W 10th Street

In the late 1950s a song factory that once housed the Almanac Singers, a left-leaning group that included Woody Guthrie, Pete Seeger and Sis Cunningham.

Americana Hotel   811 7th Avenue

Venue of a rather grudging acceptance by Dylan of a Tom Paine Award.

The Beacon Theatre*   2124 Broadway

The venue that Dylan has played most. Musical home from home (see page 129).

Belasco Theater*   111 W 44th Street

Broadway home of the Conor McPherson play *Girl From The North Country*, which began in London in 2017. Production reopened in June 2021.

Big Pink   56 Parnassus Lane, West Saugerties, New York, 12477

The Band's infamous upstate refuge, a creative play space where *The Basement Tapes* were recorded in 1967, and the Band's Music from Big Pink in 1968. The homeowners, we're told, are friendly – but don't knock, be courteous, and whatever you do, don't wander. The neighbours are wary.

The Bitter End/The Other End*   147 Bleecker Street

It may have been renamed (in 1975), but this venue's the rare entry to remain essentially unchanged. It's still a rollicking music venue and bar. Dylan hung here well into the '70s, where management helped shield him from the public. He shot pool with Kris Kristofferson, etc. (see page 97).

Bottom Line   15 W 4th Street

Important Greenwich Village venue.

Sis Cunningham's apartment/   104th Street Brooks
***Broadside* magazine**

Broadside magazine (very influential in the folk-revival) was the first time Dylan's work was in print and the magazine was the first to publish 'Blowin' in the Wind' in 1962. Contributors met monthly at the apartment.

Cafe Bizarre   106 W 3rd Street

Folk Club opened in1957. Now an NYU Law School Building.

Cafe Figaro   184 Bleecker Street

Originally called Le Figaro Cafe. Closed since 2008. In January 2021, it was announced that the cafe would be reopening in the same location sometime in the spring or summer as Figaro Cafe.

Cafe Wha?*   115 MacDougal Street

Legendary music venue (see page 9).

Caffé Dante*   79–81 MacDougal Street

Now Dante NYC. Originally opened in 1915, when Greenwich Village was called 'South Village" and was primarily Italian.

Caffé Lena*   47 Phila Street, Saratoga Springs, NY

Early music venue for Dylan and still going (see page 47).

Caffe Reggio* 119 MacDougal Street

Cosy cafe and restaurant. May or may not have introduced cappuccino to New York City.

Carnegie Chapter Hall 881 7th Ave

Location of Dylan's first concert, for which 53 tickets were sold.

Chip Monck's basement apartment Underneath the Village Gate

At the corner of Thompson and Bleecker Streets. The location for Dylan's sofa surfing location and important for the loan of Chip's typewriter (see page 53).

Columbia's Studio A* 799 7th Ave

Dylan recorded many albums here through the 1960s, including *The Freewheelin' Bob Dylan*, *Highway 61 Revisited* and *Blonde on Blonde*. *Another Side of Bob Dylan* was recorded here on one day, on 8 August 1964. In December 1964, 'according to Sound Engineer Jim Reeves, with producer Tom Wilson, he experimented with a 'Fats Domino early rock n roll thing' over 'House of the Rising Sun'. It was discarded.

On 29 September 1961, this was the location of Dylan's first professional recording on an album with Carolyn Hester.

The Commons/ Fat Black Pussycat
105 MacDougal Street

Here, we are told, Dylan wrote 'Blowin' in the Wind'. The space changed hands and became Fat Black Pussycat (now located at 130 W 3rd Street, and still featuring a performance space). 105 MacDougal's been a Mexican restaurant for years now, Panchito's Mexican Cantina. The food's okay.

Dave Van Ronk and Terri Thal's apartment
190 Waverly Place

Location of important evenings with Bob, Suze, Dave and Terri (see page 47).

Delmonico Hotel*(now renamed)
502 Park Avenue

Host to the first meeting between Dylan and the Beatles in 1964 (see page 55). Donald Trump acquired the property in 2001 and renamed it the Trump Park Avenue. It's still a hotel, so maybe … get a drink at the bar.

Dylan Liberation Front Offices
E 12th Street

Headquarters for A.J. Weberman's campaign (see page 90).

Dylan townhouse, 'Strivers' Row', Harlem
265 W 139th Street.

A Dylan residence for 14 years, finally sold in the year 2000.

Dylan's apartment with Suze 161 W 4th Street
Important early home for Dylan (see page 36).

Dylan's home with Sara and family 94 MacDougal Street

Dylan's Recording Studio 124 W Houston Street
Between Sullivan and Thompson. Dylan rented out the ground floor as a studio from conceptual artists Arakawa and Madeline Gins. There are two entrances, the right-hand door was Dylan's. Back in 2013, a tenant discovered in an upstairs closet 146 acetate records from the studio sessions for *Nashville Skyline*, *New Morning* and *Self-Portrait*.

A.J. Eighth Street Bookshop 32 W 8th Street, 17 8th Street
Closed since '79. Now a coffee shop, Stumptown Coffee Roasters. But if you're looking for a Village bookstore, check out Three Lives & Company at 154 W 10th Street, a favourite of Allen Ginsberg's. Don't let the size of the shop fool you: they have one of the most thoughtfully curated fiction collections in the city.

The Factory 231 E 47th Street
Andy Warhol's studio, the site of his creative HQ.

The Five Spot   St Mark's Place & 3rd Ave

Originally at 5 Cooper Square (now a bank), then at 2 St Mark's Place. Pioneering Jazz Club where Dylan saw Thelonius Monk. He said of Monk that he 'summoned magic shadows into being'.

Folklore Center   110 MacDougal Street

Focal point of the Village. Established by Izzy Young (see page 32).

Folkways Records   165 W 46th Street

Important folk music publishers.

The Freewheelin' Bob Dylan   Jones Street facing North between Bleecker and W 4th

Site of the famous album cover for *The Freewheelin' Bob Dylan*, photographed by Don Hunstein (see page 43).

Gaslight Cafe   116 MacDougal Street

Coffeehouse opened in 1958. Also known as the Village Gaslight and fictionalised in the TV series *The Marvelous Mrs Maisel*. It closed in 1971.

Live at The Gaslight 1962 is an album of Dylan performances here in October 1962.

Gerde's Folk City   11 W 4th Street Gramercy Park

One of the most important Village Folk clubs (see page 19).

Lexington Ave Groove*   125 MacDougal Street

Mural of famous artists associated with the Village.

Hotel Chelsea*   222 W 23rd Street

Famous hotel and occasional Dylan bed (see page 53).

Hotel Earle now renamed   103 Waverly Place
Washington Square Hotel*

Important location for both the Dylan and the Greenwich Village story (see page 55).

Kettle of Fish*   59 Christopher Street

Originally at 114 MacDougal Street, above the Gaslight, then at 130 W 3rd Street, now at 59 Christopher Street (see page 69).

Leeds Music Publishing   Upper West Side

Site of Dylan's first publishing contract.

Madison Square Garden*   4 Penn Plaza

Famous concert hall and venue for Night of The Hurricane (see page 115).

Marlton Hotel 5 W 8th Street

This former flophouse is now a posh hotel: they've gone to great lengths to memorialise the building's history. Besides Dylan, there's a long list of literary regulars. Kerouac wrote *Subterraneans* and *Tristessa* here.

Mell and Lilian Bailey's apartment 183 East 3rd Street

Sofa surfing location (see page 137).

Minetta Tavern* 113 MacDougal Street

This Italian restaurant is a legendary Greenwich Village watering hole (see page 56).

Music Inn* 169 W 4th Street

Next door to the apartment Dylan shared with Suze Rotolo. It still hosts open mic nights every Thursday. Or it did ... and surely will, pandemic pending (see page 37).

New York Public Library* 5th Ave at 42nd Street

Early Dylan educational location (see page 66).

Newspaper Kiosk on Sheridan Square

Located on the far West side of Christopher Street Park, above the Christopher Street subway station, on Seventh Avenue South. Bob and Suze rushed here to get the early editions of the career-changing Robert Shelton *New York Times* review.

People's Songs office　　　　　130 W 42nd Street

Peter Seeger's HQ (see page 30).

Philharmonic Hall　　　　　132 W 65th Street

Music venue, Dylan played here on 31 October 1964.

Power Station* 　　　　　441 W 53rd Street

Opened in 1977. Dylan recorded the *Infidels* album here and outtakes which include the classic 'Blind Willie McTell'.

Riverside Church* 　　　　　490 Riverside Drive

The Hootenanny where Bob met Suze (see page 41).

Sheridan Square Playhouse,　　　　　99 7th Ave S
the Garage Restaurant & Cafe

Location were Dylan saw rehearsals for the George Tabori play *Brecht on Brecht* in 1962. Suze Rotolo was working as the Production Designer on the play.

Sis Cunningham and Gordon　　　　　W 104th Street
Friesen's apartment

Founders in 1962 of *Broadside* magazine. The words of 'Blowin' in the Wind' were published with a picture of Dylan on the cover, May 1962.

Sony Music Studios*　460 W 54th Street Studio 50

Recording studios, location for *MTV Unplugged* in November 1994.

Ed Sullivan Theater* 1697–99 Broadway

Venue for Dylan TV performance (see page 118).

Supper Club, Hotel Edison* 228 W 47th Street

On 16–17 November 1983, Dylan played four intimate concerts, considered by many to be among his finest live performances.

Suze and Carla Rotolo's apartment 106 Ave B & E 7th Street

Early and very important sofa surfing location.

Theater de Lys (renamed 121 Christopher Street
Lucille Lortel Theater)

A 1926 Theater distinguished for remaining unstained by the generations of ambitious renovators with more money than taste.

Dylan said in *Chronicles Vol. 1*: In a few years' time, I'd write and sing songs like 'It's Alright Ma (I'm Only Bleeding)', 'Mr Tambourine Man' … 'Hard Rain's a-Gonna Fall' and some others like that. If I hadn't gone to the Theater De Lys and heard the (Brecht) ballad 'Pirate Jenny' it might not have dawned on me to write them, that songs like this could even be written.

Town Hall 123 W 43rd Street

A mainstay for intimate shows whenever Dylan tours through town. Next door, at 101 W 43rd Street, stood the Hanover House Hotel, another tenant hotel long since demolished and where Woody Guthrie first stayed after he hitchhiked to Manhattan in 1940. In his room here he wrote 'This Land Is Your Land'.

Tuscarora Reservation*   2006 Mt Hope Road, Lewistown, NY State

Stopping point on the Rolling Thunder Revue.

Village Gate   158 Bleeker Street

Closed since 1994. The building retains the Gate's original street sign. The upstairs Theater now houses (Le) Poisson Rouge, a music venue and performance space. Downstairs there's another pharmacy.

Village Vanguard*   178 7th Ave

A Greenwich Village mainstay since 1935. Still a great place for jazz in the city. Intimate and alive.

Washington Square Park*

The beating heart of Greenwich Village (see page 61).

White Horse Tavern*   567 Hudson Street

Legendary Greenwich Village bar (see page 63).

Whitmark & Sons   488 Madison Ave

Publishing company and location for early Dylan demo recordings between 1962–64 (later released as a Bootleg Series album).

Woody Guthrie Foundation 125–31 E Main St, Mount Kisco NY

The site of the Woodie Guthrie archives.

Woody Guthrie House 3520 Mermaid Ave on Coney Island, Brooklyn NY

Location for many a folk pilgrimage in the early '60s.

Still open

BIBLIOGRAPHY

Bob Dylan, Anthony Scaduto (Grossat & Dunlap, 1971)

'Scuse Me While I Kiss The Sky: Jimi Hendrix: Voodoo Child, David Henderson (Doubleday & Company, 1978)

Baby Let Me Follow You Down, Eric Von Schmidt and Jim Rooney (Doubleday Press, 1979)

Edie: American Girl, Jean Stein (Grove Press, 1982)

Bound For Glory: The Hard-driving, Truth-telling, Autobiography of America's Great Poet-Folk Singer Woody Guthrie (New American Library, 1983)

No Direction Home: The Life and Music of Bob Dylan, Robert Shelton (New English Library, 1986)

All Across The Telegraph: A Bob Dylan Handbook, John Bauldie & Michael Gray (Sidgwick & Jackson, 1987)

Rock Wives: The Hard Lives and Good Times of the Wives, Girlfriends and Groupies of Rock and Roll, Victoria Balfour (William Morrow & Co, 1987)

Wanted Man: In Search of Bob Dylan, edited by John Bauldie (Black Spring Press, 1990)

Hoot! A Twenty-Five Year History of The Greenwich Village Music Scene, Robbie Woliver (St Martin's Press, 1994)

Various Positions: A Life of Leonard Cohen, Ira Bruce Nadel (Pantheon, 1994)

Down The Highway: The Life of Bob Dylan, Howard Sounes (Doubleday, 2001)

Positively 4th Street: The Lives and Times of Joan Baez, Bob Dylan, Mimi Baez Farina and Richard Farina, David Hajdu (Farrer, Strauss and Giroux, 2001)

On The Road with Bob Dylan, Larry Sloman (Crown, 2002)

Chronicles: Volume 1, Bob Dylan (Simon & Schuster, 2004)

Bluegrass: A History, Neil V. Rosenberg (University of Illinois Press, 2005)

The Bob Dylan Encyclopedia, Michael Gray (Continuum, 2006)

Ramblin' Jack Elliott: The Never-Ending Highway, Hank Reinike (American Folk Music and Musicians Series), (Scarecrow Press, 2009)

A Freewheelin' Time: A Memoir of Greenwich Village in the Sixties, Suze Rotolo (Broadway Books, 2009)

Political Folk Music in America from its Origins to Bob Dylan, Lawrence J Epstein (McFarland & Company, 2010)

Bob Dylan in America, Sean Wilentz (Vintage, 2011)

Don't Tell Me How I Looked Falling: The Ballad of Peter La Farge, Sandra Hale Schulman (Slink Productions, 2012)

The Mayor of MacDougal Street: A Memoir, Dave Van Ronk (Da Capo Press, 2013)

Caffe Lena: Inside America's Legendary Folk Music Coffee House, Jocelyn Arem, Joe Alper (PowerHouse books, 2013)

A Broken Hallelujah: Rock and Roll, Redemption and the Life of Leonard Cohen, Leil Leibovitz (Sandstone Press, 2014)

Folk City: New York and the American Folk Music Revival, Stephen Petrus and Ronald D. Cohen (OUP USA, 2015)

This Singin' Thing: Untold tales of a travelling troubadour from the 1960s, John R. Winn (CreateSpace, 2015)

Bob Dylan: Outlaw Blues, Spencer Leigh (McNidder & Grace, 2020)

Additional Resources

People's Songs, Volume 1, 1945, Volume 2 (Feb/March)

Talking Folklore Center, Jim downing, documentary film, 1989

Sunday, Dan Drasin, documentary film, 1963

Don't Make It Easy, Charlotta Hayes, documentary by Sisyfos Films, 2023

Theme Time Radio Hour www.themetimeradio.com

'Bob Dylan: A Distinctive Folk-Song Stylist', Robert Shelton (*New York Times*, September 29, 1961)

'Bob Dylan Meets The Press', Jack Goddard (*Village Voice*, March 1965)

Bob Dylan: The Charisma Kid, Robert Shelton (Fawcett, July 1965)

Nat Hentoff, *Playboy*, March 1966

Claudia Dreifus, *Rolling Stone*, 4 March 1971

'Interview at Ritz-Carlton Hotel', Bert Kleinman, 30 July 1984. Transcription in *Talkin' Bob Dylan 1984 & 1985 (Some Educated Rap)* by Stewart P. Bicker

LA Johnson Interview with Joan Baez August 1995 www.bobdylanroots.com

'When Dylan Met the Beatles – History In A Handshake, Andrew Harrison (*The Guardian*, August 27, 2014)

Bob Dylan Had An Obsessive Fan Who Always Went Through His Trash – Here's Why (The Vintage News, 28 August 2018)

Steve Earle Makes Himself at home in New York City, www.straight.com, 12 March 2008

Marvels of Modern Music Featuring Tony Glover's Bob Dylan Archives, RR Auction, 19 October 2020

Chip Monck: Melbourne man worked with Rolling Stones, Woodstock, Bob Dylan www.smh.com.au 17 August 2014

The Right to Perform Music in Washington Square Park in April – April 1961 Folk Riot and Now www.washingtonsquareparkblog.com 27 April 2015

Bob Dylan With The Plugz Play 'Jokerman' On Letterman, Rob Jones, The Delete Bin, 18 May 2015

Bob Dylan Center In Tulsa Will Open To The Public in May 2022 www.route66news.com 14 May 2021

Calle Si Blogspot, 2021

www.kettleoffishnyc.com

www.cafewha.com

www.washingtonsquarehotel.com

www.ciscohouston.com

2021 interviews with Scarlet Rivera, A.J. Weberman, Terri Thal, John Winn, Rob Stoner, Peter

MacKenzie, Judy and Marc Paul, John Sorenson, Bob Porco, Susan Blanchard Ryan, Maureen Van Zandt and Jeff Slatnick.

ACKNOWLEDGEMENTS

Thanks to Terri Thal, Dina Regine, Maureen Van Zandt, John Winn, Charlotta Hayes, Scarlet Rivera, Rob Stoner, Judy and Marc Paul, A.J. Weberman, Peter McKenzie, John Sorensen, Phil T Listener, Susan Blanchard Ryan, Anne Margaret Daniel, Michael Gray, James Adams, Harold Lepidus, Dr Salvatore Fallica, Gareth Davies, Sue Osborne, Lynda B Schneider, Stephen Petrus, Sandra Hale Schulman, Catherine Butler, Malcolm Barr-Hamilton, Tim Smith, Adam Scott Goulding, Annie Kapur, Adrienne and Tom at the Kettle of Fish and the wonderfully supportive Caroline and Andy Peden Smith from McNidder & Grace.

AUTHOR BIOGRAPHY

 **K G Miles**. Bob Dylan has taken Londoner K G Miles on an emotional musical journey lasting over 50 years, from an awestruck child at the Isle of Wight Festival in 1969 to the honour of addressing the inaugural conference at the Tulsa Archive in 2019. Now, as co-curator of the Dylan Room at London's Troubadour Club, through writing, podcasts and Dylan tours, K G Miles is able to share his knowledge and experience with music lovers throughout the world.

ALSO BY K G MILES

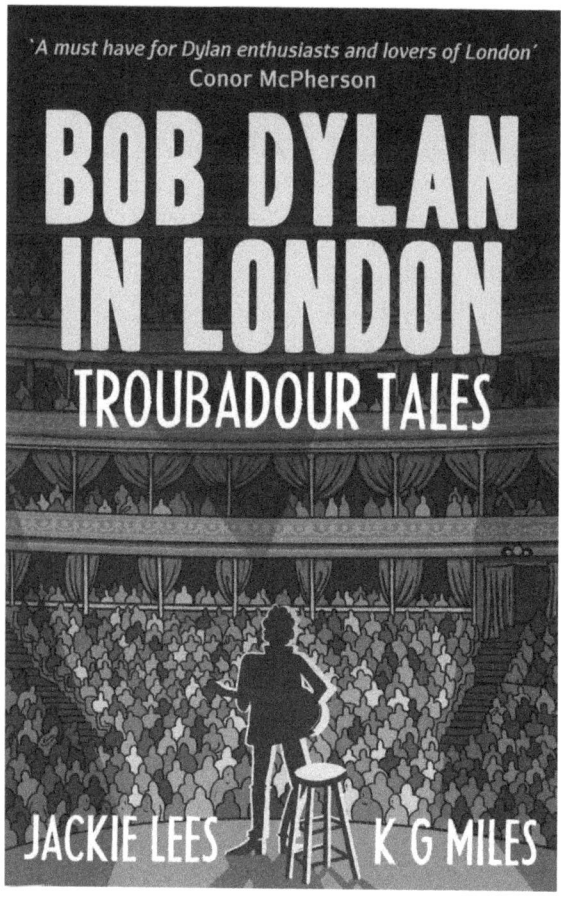

ISBN 9780857162144

'Meticulously researched and packed with delicious detail, this highly enjoyable book reveals both Bob Dylan and London in all of their compelling originality. With wry observation and entertaining incident, this is the story of Dylan's earliest visits to London as an unknown folk singer, crashing in friends' bedsits, right through to his sell-out concerts at the Royal Albert Hall and Earls Court. A must have for Dylan enthusiasts and lovers of London.'

Conor McPherson, playwright, *Girl from the North Country*

www.ingramcontent.com/pod-product-compliance
Ingram Content Group UK Ltd.
Pitfield, Milton Keynes, MK11 3LW, UK
UKHW052314160226
468107UK00005B/33